Lives Oxymoronic

Peter Seadle

DORRANCE
PUBLISHING CO
EST. 1920
PITTSBURGH, PENNSYLVANIA 15238

Dorrance Publishing Company, Inc.
585 Alpha Drive
Pittsburgh, PA 15238
Visit our website at *www.dorrancebookstore.com*

ISBN: 978-1-4809-2008-8
eISBN: 978-1-4809-2123-8

THE LUNCHEON

"The lobby of Crane's hotel," she had said.

"At seven," I had said.

"Yes, at seven."

And that is why I am here now in the lobby of this hotel, even though it is only 20 minutes to seven.

It would not really have surprised anyone who knows me because I am always early simply because I have a horror of being late.

It is, of course, silly of me. A phobia. Almost everyone with whom I have an appointment is late. I have probably spent half of my life waiting for others. Actually I think it is very strange in this age of efficiency and timetables, enforced by computer reminders and appointment calendars, that everyone is so casual about wasting my time. But then, it is only MY time they are wasting, and in the opinion of most of the world, my time is worth very little and even nothing at all. You see, I am a writer, not a very organized profession as they see it, something you can do at any time and any place. Surely, I am resourceful enough to carry paper and pencil with me at all time.

Now their time, that is quite a different matter. Their time is productive; time is money, you know. Business deals must be concluded now before someone else gets the advantage; machinery must not be allowed to slow down or it may grind to a halt. Ah, to be responsible for progress.

I have some suspicion when someone comes rushing up to me (late, of course) with an apologetic smile and explains, "So sorry. I'm much too busy unfortunately." Are they actually trying to impress upon me how important they are? How the progress of the world rests on their shoulders, and I should congratulate myself that they even make time for me?

Of course, not all of the people I deal with are of the business variety. There is the socially minded variety who say, "So sorry, simply much too involved." It seems theirs is a life of causes, and there are so many of them. Well, someone has to save the world, but it does seem strange that I have never heard of a cause to come to a happy solution. They just spawn more causes designed to attack the original problem more efficiently. Also each one feels that if they only had more funds/and so they are very busy sending letters which somewhere suggest an amount but encourages a higher donation with the phrase "this amount would help so much."

However, none of that applies to her, for whom I was waiting. It had been quite clear from our first brief meeting that she was neither too busy (pleasantly and comfortably independent due to an inheritance) nor much involved. We had met at a charity luncheon, and she had said very clearly: "Do-gooders bore me".

Maybe I need to explain how someone like me was at a luncheon of this sort in the first place. I had been invited by mistake. A very rich man and I share the same name, even the fist name, and even though we live nowhere near each other, sometimes his mail is delivered to my door by mistake. Apparently the post office is just as indifferent as I am; or have they perhaps a lot of unsuccessful poets on their staff.

Anyway, the invitation was clearly meant for him, and I went for him simply to do him an anonymous favor. People of his wealth must get at least one invitation of this sort every day, and while he may not miss the money he is expected to give, these gatherings must become a terrible bore for him. Surely he does not miss one more chicken dinner, a lukewarm cup of coffee, and an overly sweet and calorie-rich desert. Probably at the end he does not put a wad of dollar bills on the table, but makes his contribution by check later on. Chances are he does not even remember whether he was at this gathering and automatically instructs his secretary to send a check.

I of course, am in no position to contribute even a dime; in fact I could benefit from some well-meant charity myself. This, again, has something to do with the post-office. For months now I had expected an angry reminder to finally pay a goodly sum of money I had borrowed. Not all at once and not from the same source because my credit is not all that good. I had discovered that little dribbles can add up pretty fast. For a while I had ignored little hints (courteous), reminders (coldly businesslike), and stern admonitions (threats). From past experience I knew that the next missive would be a legal document that could not be ignored unless I was prepared to become a fugitive from justice. What a pleasant surprise, therefore, when instead I received a receipted bill for the entire amount with a friendly note of thanks (printed).

I realized, of course, immediately that my notes had been paid by my namesake, and most likely not out of charity but by an efficient aide who was in charge of settling bills that arrived in the central office. The amount, which was so clearly beyond me, had obviously been settled out of petty cash. Surely this kindness required an act of gratitude on my part, something I could not fulfill with a thank-you postcard. So there it was that I made my decision to repay his generosity in the same anonymous fashion by representing his (our) name at the luncheon.

A quarter past seven! This girl is too pretty to be so coldly efficient in the world of industry. So where is she?

Maybe I should have remembered that we had met at a charity affair and I should have realized that she must be at least peripherally involved with that sort of thing. Had I misinterpreted her remark to me? Was she actually so well off and involved in such affairs that she had become bored and blasé? Surely not, or she would not have talked to me at all. Not that I had experience in these circles, but I am certain girls like that can smell poverty.

Maybe there is a scheme that invites pretty girls because men would be ashamed not to contribute goodly amounts in her presence. Even I had given two dollars and said casually, "I'll send the rest later." Let them think I am eccentric.

Or, her presence might have been due to the attendance of these several very dapper young men, clean shaven, eager, all of them with heavy horn-rimmed glasses, looking as though they had been mass produced. This probably represented their effort to become a member of this affluent society by contributing way beyond their means as an investment into their future. One of these rising efficiency experts probably brought her along as a further indication of his merit. Maybe he already had a contractual arrangement with her.

There she was!!! And she smiled at me. At me!!!

"Please forgive," she said, " I have no excuse for being so late. I'll try harder the next time."

The next time!!! I was dreaming.

"By the way, we have never been formally introduced. I am Beverly."

"What a nice name. I am Frank Golden. I thought you might know my name from the nametags on the table."

"Yes, actually I do," she said. "I am Beverly Golden, and you are my father." She smiled.

I may be a poet, but words failed me. What could I say?

"I am so sorry," I finally managed. "I meant no harm. The mail..."

"I know. The mail has gotten mixed up for years. We have always enjoyed your letters, especially when we learned you had published something. But you are not very good with money, and that is why my father paid your bills."

"Is this why you are here?"

"Heavens no. We are surrounded by people who are good with money and want more of it all the time."

"You mean the well polished young men with the horn-rimmed glasses?"

"Precisely. And are you ready to have a drink now?"

I was and of this writing we have been married for 28 years and none of our three children wears glasses.

THE MONUMENT

When the famous actor Tobias Talentino died on the 12th of August 1928, there was scarcely a dry eye in the entire city. Unforgettable his Julius Cesar, his King Lear, his Ibsen interpretations, and even his many comic roles. Never again would one get to see such memorable buffoons, scoundrels and tyrants that filled you with terror and yet sympathy for centuries. Of course, Tobias himself had been neither a tyrant nor a fool, but a kindly and generous person. All right, so he was a bit conceited too, but after all he was an actor and he deserved that much.

Considering all of this, the artist Tobias Talentino had every reason to be most satisfied with his funeral. No surprise that since he himself was directing all of it in absentia from the only cloud hovering in the blue, blue sky. A long procession of well-known politicians preceded the members of the family dressed all in black. Thus it happened that Liselotte Binsenmeler, former ingénue on a provincial stage, got to play her most important major role. She knew full well that her former husband had only loved her because she was a very mediocre actress, and as such she could hardly misuse his good name to further her own career. Behind her the first and third wife both dressed very stylishly. His second wife had to miss the occasion because of a severe cold. Since her divorce had been a scandal for years, she was certain her present cold was his fault even now. Seven children followed the ladies, grouped from left to right by height and age. This arrangement Tobias had left to the to the local director, since he was rather uncertain which child was which and scarcely recognized two of the boys and the one girl. Now came various fellow actors, stage workers, and a long procession of the populace who felt they had to be present at this historic occasion. Even a couple of critics had joined the mourners.

The president of the arts council himself had thus been given the sad task to present the honorable deceased to eternity. The national symphony and the state chorus expressed the general emotion with a performance of Beethoven's ninth, and the just developing film industry did its best to cover the event for future generations. It was a dignified though somewhat lengthy festivity, and we beg your forgiveness, if we spare you all the details. When his mortal remains were finally given to the earth.

Even Tobias had grown tired, and stretched out on his comfortable cloud and promptly fell asleep. What he could not know was that all of his had come about quite naturally, because those who are expected to go to heaven are generally allowed to be present at their funeral, which may be the lone occasion when only nice things are said about him. Then, however, most of them are given an eternal rest.

Quite right, I said 'most of them'. Of course it is different for the immortals. And so it happened that after a sleep of several months the actor Tobias Binsenmeier (his real name now) suddenly had the feeling that he was about to wake up. It took several days but then he could open his eyes. Surprised he looked about and immediately recognized that he was in a studio of what seemed to be a sculptor.

We must explain. It seems that those of the citizens concerned about culture had decided to honor the great deceased with a monument. The commission had been granted to the most famous sculptor of the country, whose task it was now to reawaken the deceased in stone for all to admire forever, Of course Tobias was very, very proud since that was more than even he had expected.

With great curiosity he followed this work as he was slowly brought back to his own image out of the dead stone. Of course it tickled a bit as his noble nose was formed, again a bit under his right arm which was supposed to be raised and hold up a laurel wreath.

Too disappointing when he learned that the sculptor had not yet been paid since the collection had not met with the expected enthusiasm. Indeed the matter, for some time, reached a state of crisis, and the unfinished stone was hauled into a corner of the studio for a time. Of course, Tobias was most upset since he was the opinion that one artist must not think about payment (o.k. about taxes than) to honor his equal.

The problem was finally solved by a personal donation from his fourth wife who had already played two parts in a film on the basis of her now well-recognized name. She knew publicity had to be paid for. Naturally the sculptor had already started other assignments and thus simplified his previous design. Instead of the artistic curls, Tobias was now crowned by an old-fashioned hat he would never have worn. The lower part of the body was now just indicated, as if the artist was just rising out of the stone. That was all right with Tobias because now he would lean against the stone rather than stand forever on his own two feet.

Thus the work was soon finished when a new crisis forced him into the corner. The question as to where this statue was to be placed had not yet been solved. Not in front of the theater where he would have to compete with Shakespeare. More months passed and more committees held hearings and poor Tobias grew more and more desperate.

At last!!! Because the general temper of the times was quite anti militaristic, it was decided to rename the General von Clausewitz Square and remove the giant image of the general on a horse which had so much interfered with the traffic as the Tobias Binsenmeier Square. There he would stand for all eternity, and Tobias was most satisfied. At least he was transported from the dusty studio into the fresh air. Besides, since the celebration was almost a repetition of his original day of honor, except that this time politicians stood at the head of it all and delivered long recitations about the arts of the people, the educational role of the stage, and all sorts of nonsense like it. Since Tobias stood under a large linen cloth, he could barely follow what went on, but what he did understand was the applause when the linen was removed. He almost bowed when he remembered that he was now a monument. Someone still read the text on the brass plate mounted on the stone from which he was rising. "Tobias Talentino, nee Binsenmeier. 1857-1928. Actor. He did not play a part; he was the person he portrayed." Nonsense, of course, he thought, but he was too tired to worry about it.

Even to following days were still disturbing. First workers came, who created a narrow but attractive ring of grass with nice flowers around him. Nice enough to satisfy his sense of nature. Then one morning a whole team of cameras appeared with his former wife, no longer in black but with a dress that featured a décolletage he found excessive for her 56 years. In an interview on the grass spot she indicated that now she was also interested in playing more sexy parts (naturally discretely), which up to now she had sacrificed in honor of the name of departed husband. Tobias turned red with rage, which the film crew ascribed to the sun overhead. But in the end he just smiled since he of course knew the truth of it all from really close up.

Now life became more peaceful. Certainly others came who looked up to him, more senior citizens mostly, and for a while there was that obviously very old little lady who came once every week with a modest bunch of flowers that she placed before him, lowering her head and sighing deeply before she left again.

Both Tobias and the press soon tried to find out who she was. He never came to a satisfactory answer. Surely a flame of his young years who had guarded this precious fire for all of her life. No question, he was moved and when she no longer came he felt real grief.

Life became more and more monotonous and the nights seemed to get colder and colder. When the snow came, he was glad he had been given the large hat, but his right shoulder was ever more bothered by rheumatism since he still had to support the laurel wreath. Also the traffic had increased since the lorry driver found it easier to cross of this smaller square. The stench of gasoline became unbearable in the summer and the grassy circle was now totally neglected, because those heavy tires simply drover over it.

Then there were those children who had started to climb up to him and threw balls on him. One even took a piece of coal and painted an ugly mustache on his noble upper lip. He was glad not to have a mirror to see himself. Finally some disgusting little urchin hung on to his laurel wreath, which promptly broke off. Tobias was most satisfied that the boy fell off and broke his leg weeping loudly. Swell, at least Tobias had less to carry but then once more he felt degraded when a mother opened the pants of her little boy and directed him to pee against the stone. Dogs seem to like the idea and copied this procedure.

Thus the years ran past and the sadness over being forgotten changed to resignation. He was no longer interested in the world, even when he read in newspaper that the wind had blown in his direction; the well-known actress Liselotte Binsenmeier had married a 28-year-old singer of popular tunes. He felt nothing; he cared about nothing.

It grew almost airily quiet when one day large posters appeared that here the city was going to construct a below ground garage. It was clear to Tobias that his days here were numbered. And surely, soon a long truck appeared with a crane, pulled him out of the grow-jet somewhat harshly. For the first time in years he was interested where his voyage might lead. It ended in a park under nice large trees where other long retired statues had been placed. Even Clausewitz was there, and they might compare notes about their common home. The whole journey had last barely three hours and all of his new neighbors had been placed there without attention to rank, status, or profession. In fact, here was a collection of the entire intellectual inventory of the western world even including mythological representatives of the distant past, some of whom looked quite dilapidated.

But we have not yet reported on the best. Right next to him on a piece of marble lay a young woman with an exposed bosom. The rest of her charms where cleverly indicated as though she was simply covered by a thin veil. When he first saw he like that, he modestly closed his eyes, even though he had hardly been that way in life. She had obviously caught his glance, smiled a charming smile and said even quite clearly, "Good Morning".

"Good morning, madam," he answered somewhat hoarsely, which was partly his excitement and partly that he had not used his voice in years.

"Be glad it is all behind you; the dirt, the stench, the noise, the stupid people," she continued .

"You mean none of this exists here? Is this the paradise?"

She laughed. "No, not quite. It is simply the junk room. Seriously, you are now in what is called the Park of Western Culture. Right around the corner there are Kant, Dante, Beethoven. And the one on the three legged horse is Frederick the Great, and that large behind there under the bushes is all that is left of Helen of Troy."

"Too bad," said Tobias and realized immediately he should not have said it.

"If you think so," the lady said, somewhat offended. "Actually she is quite an insufferable person once you get to know her. By the way, I am Sappho."

"Really, really!' Tobias shouted full of enthusiasm." Then we already know each other, at least indirectly."

"Is that so? I don't seem to remember..."

"No, no, not in life. You see, I am an actor and many years ago you once loved me on the stage," he stretched the words, "in spite of it all." He saw immediately that he had made a great mistake.

"Always this 'in spite of it.' If I ever get a hold of those so called poets," she breathed heavily.

"But madam," he said, "they also gave you quite normal human feelings!"

"Nonsense!" But she seemed somewhat calmer and even wiggled slightly with her hips. "What do these bourgeois know about the normal feelings of a woman, a very woman who loves life. And sex is sex; you just have to know how to do it. Maybe you don't know that we had not all that many men, so have to learn to help yourself. In fact, I have loved just as many men as women. May we hope that the day will come when women have the same right of choice as men."

Tobias found his balance again. "Believe me, dear lady, I really loved you then and now that I came to know you even more personally; believe me, I know that I should have met you with even greater passion."

Immediately he recognized that he had found the right words, and soon they agreed that he would no longer call her 'madam' or 'dear lady', and she would call him Toby.

Life seemed idyllic in the park, and it was rare that someone came to visit. Even the doves hardly stayed around and seemed to prefer the heads of the modern politicians. But Toby quickly found his way among the luminaries. He arranged theatrical evenings for which Socrates and Lope da Vega furnished the texts. On beautiful fall evenings there always was a choral concert that Beethoven had arranged and for which even the military voices proved their usefulness, since they had been trained to be well understood in commanding. Still it was a sad existence since the world knew nothing of the spirit so close among them, which displayed its talents during the dark off night, since they had to return to their stone base with the first rays of light. Yet, this could have become an eternity if the now dominating technologic civilization had not put an end to it all. What now appeared were not the large trucks, but huge destructive machines that muscular men used to smash not only the statues but mashed the stone bases, the trees of the park, the grass, the earth to construct what a big sign now informed the world. Here your city is constructing your new 3 story underground garage! No evidence was left of stony reminder of a dead culture, which had been ground into cement.

Now Toby had come to the end of his suffering. Now he could sleep and only occasionally he woke up with his old friends and together they look down. At times a gentle soul who wanted to be born floated past them and with very soft voices they wished it good luck.

"Don't become immortal," they advised, "it is not worth it." But those souls who do not come from the heavens but from below; they deserve it if some day they become a monument.

REUNION

The disagreeable part of travel is the fellow travellers sitting next to you. Of course one should always be polite and ask, "Is this place free?" or perhaps even offer a "Good morning," but this gesture of good manners, should not by any means be understood as an invitations to a public exchange of intimate details of one's life. Please don't misunderstand and assume I have something against people in general. I love to look out of the window and watch how their lives take place as we race past. There, on the highway, a man is walking along. Where does he want to go? Why? And now there is the fellow in his car who seems bound and determined to keep pace with the train. Is he imagining he is a frustrated race driver? Now a young couple hand in hand in the forest. Good luck to them if this is a budding romance. So much to keep me busy.

But it is rare that I can follow my imagination to its conclusion in this world of sociological wisdom with its mania for interpretation of everything. Their pronouncements tell us that an individual sitting in silence with his own thoughts is an unhappy, lonely, abandoned human being who must be saved from himself. 'Aha,' my travel companions seem to conclude, he does not read a paper; he does obviously not busily review office records in preparation for an important meeting. He is just sitting there and surely hopes for a contact but is too shy to start himself. I'll save him from himself and talk to him.

This sort of salvation generally has two different approaches. I am quizzed as to my origin and just what I do to earn my living. Does that sort of thing pay well? It must really quite agreeable to travel so freely around the world without being confined to a desk and having a wife and children watch you all the time.

As soon as I have recognized the beginning of this sort of conversational drift, I have prepared a series of answers for myself, which are designed to satisfy all desires for the discovery of a hidden sensationalism on the part of the questioner. I declare that I am only here by chance "You see I just happened to be on the station to buy a newspaper and there I found this ticket. I am not even sure were this train is going."

"Really?" is usually the only reaction I get.

But I don't take the chance that this might lead to a new inquiry, and so I deliver my coup de grace: "No, I never stay in a hotel, but I know a good brothel where I generally go which belongs to a friend of the family, a pimp, you know. Well, you know, it's really a good thing such places exist. At one time, my wife also was... well, you know. And I don't really miss the children since one can never really know whether they are your own."

With this answer I create many weeks of outrage among my travel companions, provide them with a certain dosage of deliciously satisfying superior moral thrill when they report on their travel experiences at home, and am the occasion for long dinner conversations as an example of the depravity in the world of today. Prim-looking elderly ladies frequently, immediately change their seats, while clergymen start to make notes about next Sunday's sermon. However, to tell the truth, it is not uncommon that I seem to be envied. But I rather prefer the other way of playing this game, because in this way I only need to nod, occasionally say something such as, "Is that so? or "You don't say?" In this relationship the other one starts to unpack, completely. Not his suitcase, mind you, but his life. Illnesses are quite generally the favorite subject matter, and it is quite clear that all physicians practicing today have had insufficient training or are complete lying idiots, whereas this particular laymen as well as most of his friends and relatives are in possessions of a great wealth of medical expertise. Most of the time it is rather unclear what it is that has kept my travel companions alive this long.

Photographs of happily smiling children also often play a great role. These are generally grandchildren, and they are all quite brilliant and some day they will probably save the world. Surprising how many grandmothers whose daughters are responsible for these budding geniuses will inform me about every detail of the difficult birth and, believe it or not, about the arduous process of procreation their daughter had to endure. Something like this: "They tried so hard for about five years and nothing. Naturally it was not the fault of my Kathy. I always said her husband, Sherman, was not the right man, even long before they were married. But you know about children today, they rarely pay any attention to their parents. So finally she went to see a doctor who gave her one of those Swedish pills, but that didn't help either. He, Sherman, should have gone. But then, finally it worked out after all, and in spite of the difficult birth the child, thank the Lord, seems to be healthy. Of course, you never know, such things often show up later in life. Sherman, you know, but we hope for the best."

Now this sort of travel companion at least leaves me time for my own fantasies, even though I am in this case not the determiner of the course of events. I have visions of Kathy and Sherman copulating frantically in their bed with an embroidered framed motto on the wall above them with the legend: "We must make a grandson for Sherman's mother in law!" Or I see the doctor who looks with lecherous eyes at the well developed Kathy and says, "Well, of course I could give you one of those Swedish pills...but perhaps before that you might like to try with me to...No?... Well, never mind, no harm done, just asking." I always have difficulties to suppress that inward smile while on the outside I must maintain an expression of understanding sympathy for my travel companion's problem.

For all of these reasons it was most surprising that this time I sat in my train and was hardly able to avert my eyes from my travel companion. He was a man, not very healthy looking, most likely somewhat older than I, but in general not very remarkable. Nevertheless...something gave me a feeling and made me wish fervently that he would start a conversation with me to help me determine just what it was about him. Somehow I had the feeling that I knew him, but he kept reading his newspaper, completely disinterested in me, read the news, the sports pages, and even the advertisements with great concentration.

"Please forgive me!" Those were my words and they hung in the air as though I had made some loud and obscene remark in a church. Never before had I noticed how awful my voice sounded.

The man looked up. "Yes, please?" It was too late to save myself; he had heard me and realized that I had spoken to him.

"Please forgive me," I unnecessarily repeated myself. "Don't we know each other? From somewhere? Many years ago?"

To my great surprise, he nodded." Yes," he said, "we went to the same school. I recognized you right away, but I was not sure that it would be of interest to you."

Not be of interest to me? Here was someone whose beginnings were the same as mine! For many years we undoubtedly went our different ways, but we both started from the same point, and so we had something in common. Surely it would be most interesting to know how each of us had gotten to where we were now. Here we confront the truth that represents how a life is lived in reality. You might say that here we meet the imagination of fate itself.

I opened up like a waterfall and talked and talked about myself. Never would I have imagined myself capable of this degree of voluntary intimacy with a comparative stranger. My innermost feelings kept secret for many a year were revealed here, my wrecked first marriage, my inadequate relationship with my children, worries about my job, and my disgust with the whole business climate that ruled my existence.

Naturally, as one does in situations of this sort, I would I sometimes exaggerate my successes, because I wanted him to have the impression that our common education had been worth its while, and that a bad pupil such as I had been could nevertheless succeed in life. I elevated myself from a bourgeois existence into the lower rungs of wealth, however without wanting to brag, as I assured him. Since I wanted to demonstrate that someone with our education was naturally not only interested in economic comfort, I made remarks about concerts I had never heard, about books which I only knew by title, about philosophical and religious concerns that were supposedly much on my mind.

I went on like this for at least half and hour without ceasing. He had folded his newspaper, and sometimes chimed in with a, "Yes, yes, I know how that is," but he never interrupted me with a single question. Finally, however I became aware just how grotesque this situation had become. My red face was now no longer the result of my eagerness to talk, but an embarrassment to have revealed myself so completely. If only I could have jumped through the window right here and now, but the train traveled too fast. There was only one way out to direct the attention away from my own person. It had to be his turn.

"And you?" I asked, and at the same time I wondered just what his name might be. "What happened to you?"

My inquiry seemed to be met by an endless silence. Carefully the man folded his newspaper some more. In any other circumstance I surely would have noticed how disagreeable this question was to him. "Well, you know how it is," he said. "You live and make the best of it as well as you can."

I should have noticed the meaning of this generalizing non-answer, but I became a monster. "Well now, after school, what did you do then?" I kept pressing on, and paid absolutely no attention to his sigh.

"The war, you know," he said slowly. "Like everyone else."

"But you got through it all right, didn't you?" I insisted like the worst of those offenders who in the past had selected me as their victim.

"Yes, yes, quite well," he admitted. He probably recognized that there was no way for him, and while his speech now became a bit more fluid, he expressed himself as though he were deep in thought, as if this was the very first time that he took a look at his own life. Only later did it come to me that he had dwelled on nothing but external matters.

War! Because of some sort of heroic action in the Ardennes promoted to officer status, after that as prisoner of war with much time for reading and study. Following liberation at the end of the war study at the university... Mathematics... Perhaps I could remember that he had always been quite good in math... Now still at the university but as Professor...Family, two children...a nice house in the suburbs with a large garden...all in all a quiet life. He almost seemed to excuse himself that he had nothing more exciting to tell.

"But man!" I almost shouted (it had been years that I had called anybody 'man'). "That's an absolutely brilliant success. A really totally straight path from your early interests to good grades and finally to the university as Professor of Mathematics. Something both practical and abstract to which you have devoted your life. Surely your students must feel your own love for your mission in life."

His reaction to my enthusiasm was no more than a tired wave of his hand. "Just let it be," he said. "It is really not worth talking about."

Just as I was about to protest I noticed that our train was about to arrive at our station. As we were both standing up to put on our coats my imagination again began to work, but in a somewhat strange and disturbing manner. I had a vision of my class mate in the circle of his eager students, how he explained the most difficult abstract problems in an almost unassuming manner, how they admired his knowledge, how his respectful neighbors greeted him on his way home with a friendly wave of the hand, how he entered his comfortable house with the splendid view outside of the city. Then, his family in which there were no conflicts, the hours working at his desk close to the window where he would sit for a long time deep in thought in order to determine the precisely organized mathematical coherence of the whole world, to prove the connectedness of all things, and in this manner to reveal the creator of the universe himself.

It was not enough for me to know all of these matters only in my imagination. I needed to confirm it; I needed for once in my life to bring together the imaginary and the real, and in so doing to confirm my own inner psyche.

I forced myself on him. "Perhaps we could get together somewhere for a nice comfortable evening, maybe over dinner," I pressed on. "I am certain there is still a lot we could tell each other. How we felt, what we thought at this or that point in out lives. There must still be so much..." I was hoping, no, I was insisting that he invite me to his house.

"I'd really like to have you over," he finally gave in, "but unfortunately my family is still away on vacation in the mountains. Besides, the painters are there and everything is much upset. We would have to meet somewhere else, if that might even be possible. It is such a busy time of the year for me and there are so many obligations right now."

I seemed to hear none of this and simply would not give in. At last we arranged that we would meet for dinner on Sunday evening in my hotel, the best in the city, He finally agreed and we shook hands as we parted.

In spite of the fact that it was a busy week, the days seemed to pass very slowly. Several times I was almost tempted simply to take a cab to the university where he surely had his office, but I could not know whether he might not be too busy, lecturing or something, and I wanted to experience his sphere of activity together with him.

On the following Saturday I was finally free of all business appointment and should have gone home. But there was this date we had made for the following evening so that it would be more sensible to stay here over the week end. I considered telephoning my wife, but then I would have had to explain my momentary compulsion to know more about this man. A telegram would be better which would simply state that I would be home the following Monday. I quickly wrote out the text of my message and took it to the post office, which was right around the corner.

Of course, there was a line as always, and I had to wait. Terrible, the burden they put on the shoulders of too few postal employees. The hands of the man who took my telegram trembled from exhaustion as he bent down to count the words. Suddenly, with a quite determined motion he looked up fully at me and stated a sum and ... for the first time I could look fully in his face—- Yes, it was my school mate!

So that was his real life! That is how the truth looked. I felt myself blushing deeply as I handed him the money, but I said not a word, I was too shaken up. When he gave me my change he merely said very softly, "Thank you," and right away the person behind me pushed me away from the window.

I took a long walk to reestablish my equilibrium. I accused myself for my own persistence. I recognized how I had forced him to talk with me, and how my own story had seduced him to give a false picture of himself. It was very late when I returned to my hotel, but exhausted as I was I fell asleep almost immediately.

During breakfast I tried to consider the entire matter once again in the hope of doing it with a clearer head now. Perhaps it would be best for me to leave. Surely he would not show up for our dinner date. Yet, perhaps he would. Perhaps he had not really recognized me, and all of this was only my own imagination because I had thought about him so much during the entire week. Maybe a Doppelganger? Maybe he had a twin brother. Besides, how awful would it really be if he were not a professor? Perhaps I should go to the post office and excuse myself?

In any case, I did not leave town, and when the time came for our dinner reservation, I made my way to the dining room. When I gave my name to the head-waiter, he said, " Oh, just one second," and then produced a letter that had been left there for me.

Yes, it was from him, it had to be. I tore open the envelope and read, "Dear Friend," he had written, "I have inquired and know that you are still here in this hotel, and I assume that you might even be waiting for me. Of course, I will not be there, and surely you know by now why that is so. But please do not blame yourself for anything, because I must thank you. You have given me one of the most wonderful weeks of my entire life, a week during which one man believed that I live a satisfying and satisfactory life. Several times during the last few days I went out to the university late in the evening, and there lived my own imagined life, that I had pretended for you. In fact, I plan to continue to do so ever so often, and I thank you most sincerely for the illusion of a life with meaning. A meeting with you at this time could only destroy these dreams for me."

I finished our meal all by myself, and later managed to catch a late train home. It was already dark outside, and because of the late hour I had the seat to myself.

ERNEST

It was still relatively quiet, but he knew that ten minutes later the place would be filled with the happy noises of a beginning school year. He had gotten to recognize it as a special sound in those years that he had been teaching here. The first day after a long summer, kids shouting greetings to each other, confusion, excitement, nervousness, all of this made up a special cacophony. Ernest remembered when he had come here on his first day as a teacher. He too had been nervous when he realized that for the first time this group of young people would be totally his responsibility for the next year. Would they like him? Would he like them? Would they think him too strict, too lenient, could he win their respect and their trust? Well, those fears were long behind him. All one must now guard against was that it did not become too routine. Students notice that sort of thing. But by this time he no longer needed to worry. He knew he was a good teacher, a popular teacher, whose popularity was not the result of pandering for friendship. There were certain colleagues who tried so hard to give the impression of living on the same level as their students, who spoke to them in most familiar ways. That was not in Ernest's character, not with children, and not with grown ups.

His first words to his new class had been well worked out. In past years he had written them into a small notebook, polished them, added some thoughts and eliminated others, but now he recited them by heart. What he hoped to achieve with this little lecture was that students would be aware that he loved his job, that he was honestly glad to see them, and that he hoped he would be able to help them to reach new insights in the next few months. "You never know where you will land," he generally said, "at some earlier days in my own life I had wanted to be a fireman, a subway trainman, and later a pilot."

Even though that was not quite as true as he pictured it, he went on, "The trouble is that I get dizzy on ladders, and many trains now are run by computers. So, I am sure you also have some plans and ideas for your life and that is important, one needs a vision of oneself. But it is also important that you don't settle too firmly in your early dreams. Life has a way of destroying them. Therefore, the most important thing is to remain open to many possibilities, to be prepared to study and to learn as much as you can so that you may be flexible for the future. At this point he often wondered whether they were really listening. "And, of course, you can always come and talk to me," he went on. "School does not have to stop the moment the last bell is rung."

He had no idea how his students took this lengthy dissertation. If the truth be known, he himself had lately wondered whether his delivery had not become a bit mechanical. Still, he refused to drop the matter, because in part those admonitions were for him too. After having stood here year after year he had begun to wonder whether there might not be another life for him too. Would they notice it in his voice, in his delivery/that he was somewhat like a tired actor who had spoken his lines too many times? Perhaps he should re-work his speech. Next year, for sure. After all, a teacher is something like a preacher and an actor rolled into one.

As a matter of fact, this time he felt that his audience really had listened. Apparently it had not been all that bad. So, on to the next thing, to learn to match their names and their faces. Not always an easy job, but he knew that nothing was as disturbing to students than a teacher who after the third meeting of the class had to say, "You, back there...no, the one next to you..." The other thing he had learned was to have his students say their names out loud. That way he knew how to pronounce them. At the beginning he had learned the names before they had said them out loud, and when he said them there had often been great hilarity because of mistakes he had made in pronunciation.

He concentrated hard as he listened to each one: Almers, Hank; Altman, Frank; Dormin, Susanna; etc., etc. There were 32 in his class, and each time he smiled at the newcomer and said, "'Thank you". As they heard their own voices, the atmosphere became more relaxed. He heard some giggling in the back, but it did not matter now. "Wolltin, Ernest," a somewhat pale, slight boy had said it. He had said it rather softly, but Ernest Batcher had the sense that the name had been shouted at him, loud and even challenging. "Wolltin?" he asked, quite unnecessarily, "with two l's?" The boy answered, "Yes, with two".

He no longer heard the other names, just as he no longer saw faces. Later on he did not even remember whether he had said, "Thank you," and was uncertain how he had gotten to the end of this day of school. Only one sound dominated his entire consciousness: Wolltin.

It could be a matter of chance, although it was not a name that one heard at any street corner, Still, there must be several families called Wolltin, not only the one to which Martha Wolltin belonged. And even if this boy came from such a family, it had to be his father whose name was Wolltin and not his mother. Surely by this time Martha Wolltin had married and her name would now be something quite different, something like Smith or Brown. 'It should have been Batcher' he thought suddenly, 'Mrs. Ernest Batcher'. The thought startled him when he remembered that the boy's first name was also Ernest. Still, it was probably just an accident. The name Ernest was not all that rare, no reason why it should have anything to do with him.

Then he remembered that Martha had often told him that she rather liked his name. She thought it fit him. How long ago was that, sixteen years or so? "You are so earnest," she had said to him, "sometimes too earnest." In fact, that was precisely what she had said when she had kissed him the first time. Yes, she had kissed him, because on his own he would never have found the courage, even though it was undoubtedly very clear that that was what he wanted most in this entire world. They had both been students, they were young; life was still ahead of them with all its expectations and secrets. Neither had any really grandiose plans. He wanted to be a teacher, she a nurse. How often they had walked along that little river and talked about how they wanted to be of use, each in his own way. She would heal the sick; he would help children on their road into life. There was nothing more important one could do. They had so little money at the time, yet it seemed to him now that he had been richer during those times than at any time later in his life. They made do, and when he had his first job they managed to rent rooms in the same house. And it all seemed as though it would be forever, so natural that the thought of marriage was really never mentioned.

Now, even after all this time, he still failed to understand why not. He hated that part of his memory, because he knew that it had been his fault. It had seemed irresponsible to make a commitment of this sort before he was firmly settled in a position, one that brought with it security, prospects, all those things that would be a foundation for a secure life for them and their children. Of course, children, too, for whose future one also had to be responsible. She had even offered at one time that he could take a leave from his present job, that she would be glad to support them both until he had finished work on a doctorate. It was an arrangement that was not at all unusual in this day and age. "Not for me," he had said. "I could not accept that a woman supported me." Now, that he looked back on it, this whole attitude seemed incredibly stupid. What in the world had possessed him to talk that way? Had he thought it would do damage to his manhood?

When a promising teaching job was offered to him in a bigger town 350 miles away, it seemed that here was the realistic hope for the sort of future he had envisioned. Unfortunately, Martha's mother had fallen rather ill just at that moment, so that she could not join him right away. Perhaps it was all for the best, and he could devote himself full time to his new career so that when she could come to join him he would be well settled. Once she came to visit him, but it had not been a very successful weekend, He had volunteered for certain duties at the school, and there was little time for them alone together. She promised to come back on another weekend, but it never seemed to work out. Of course, they wrote letters, at first quite regularly, and then more sporadically, until at last there was only silence. Finally, for Christmas he had managed to arrange time for a visit to her, and even today he could still feel the pain that had gripped him, when her landlady informed him that Miss Wolltin had left two or three months ago. As far as she knew, her mother had passed away, and 'no' there was no letter for him. He tried to discover where she had gone, but it was to no avail. Some of her friends acted as though they knew, but seemed unwilling to tell him. Gradually he recognized that they had little sympathy for his search. Painful as it was, he had to admit to himself that it had been his fault that she was gone.

And now there was this boy, this child with the rare name and his own first name. Was it possible that this boy...? He did not even dare to think it. To be honest, yes, it was possible, although at the time he would never have believed it. He now remembered that when she had come to visit him, she had looked rather pale and indicated that she did not feel too well. He should have listened; surely she had wanted to tell him something important, and he had just assumed it was a cold.

His guilty imagination started to work overtime. He could now imagine how she had felt at that time. Of course she had been too proud to confront him with the truth. No doubt she did not want him to think that in this way she wanted to force his hand and propose an immediate marriage. Was that why her friends had all been so curt when he inquired about her?

Once more in his mind he studied the boy's features, which had firmly impressed himself the moment he had said his name. Were they in any way like his own? Oh Lord, he never knew when people said this or that child looks just like his father or his mother. He had always agreed, although he could never see it himself, except when there were obvious signs, red hair, or something like that. But he and this boy... or did he perhaps look like his mother? In his memory he searched for her picture, which at one time had been so firmly fixed in his mind. But since then it had faded; the remembrance was still very clear, but the image?

It was already early in the morning when he came to the conclusion that all this remembering and speculating was useless. The boy existed, and this was a fact from which he now had to start. No doubt there were possibilities to trace his story. Just to do something at this late hour, he paged through the telephone book. Nothing. But that did not necessarily mean anything. The family might have moved here recently. But why did they move just to this town? Had she been looking for him, and then deliberately sent her son to this school because she knew that he taught there? What did that mean? Was it friendly; was this some sort of revenge?

At last it occurred to him that there must be registration forms at the school where one can read something about the parents. Surely that would give him an answer. But it was 4 o'clock in the morning, and he would have to wait until at least 7:30 when the secretary opened the office. He should probably also be careful, not seem too eager. Probably he would do better to wait until after the first or second period, and then casually go and pretend he needed to look up something about his new class. Nobody would suspect anything then.

It seemed like the longest night he had ever tossed and turned so restlessly. And after that, those first two classes had never seemed to end. He forced himself not to look closely at the boy Ernest or to speak to him directly. Normally he tried to get his students involved, urged them to talk, to participate, but not today. He could not talk to the others and perhaps laugh with them and ignore this one.

Finally it was time. He had planned the moment carefully. He forced himself to whistle just a bit as he casually walked down the hall to the office. In fact, he even stopped at this and that door to talk to one or the other colleague, and finally went into the office.

"Oh, yes," the secretary said. "Right over there are all the records except one."

"Who is that?" he asked, although he already knew the answer.

"A boy called... wait a moment... ah, here, a boy called Wolltin, Ernest Wolltin." Some lady, she assumed it was the mother, had promised on the phone to bring the forms as soon as possible. She had just moved to town and couldn't do it day before yesterday because she had to report to a new job."

Ernest tried to control himself. "No, matter," he said casually, "as long as I have the rest of them," and then he almost ran back to his class. Thank heavens, for a few more minutes he would be alone. He had a terrible headache, and he had learned nothing. And he would have to wait, because he could not go to the office every day and ask whether this boy 's forms had arrived. The secretary had said "the mother." Did that mean there was no father? Of course there was, he knew full well who the father was.

When a whole week had gone by without any news, he felt justified to ask again. It seemed that still nothing had been heard from the mother. "We'll send her a reminder," the secretary said, but then it turned out that they did not even have an address. "Why don't you ask the boy where he lives?" she suggested. Of course, he should have thought about that himself.

After the last class he asked Ernest whether he could stay for just a moment. The boy looked up at him in some astonishment.

"You do have a moment, don't you?" the teacher asked.

"Yea, sure," was the answer.

"Here, why don't we both sit down?" He started the conversation, hoping it all sounded informal. "I just wondered where you went to school last year. We don't seem to have that information," he asked.

The boy named a city at the other end of the country.

"That far away? Well, and where do you live now?"

"Why, here, of course."

"Yes, of course, I mean what is your address?"

The boy named a street and a number not very far from the school.

So close by, could she really be so close by?

"So, tell me, did you like your teacher in your last school?"

The boy Ernest shook his head. "Not really. But he also wasn't all that bad."

"I see. But surely it is better if one likes his teachers, don't you think?"

"Yes, I suppose."

This conversation was not going anywhere.

During the next couple of weeks he managed to sit in his car in front of her house in the hope that she might be coming home. People went in and out of the house, but never Martha.

She could not have changed so much that he would not recognize her. Finally he gave it up for fear that someone would wonder about this person sitting in his car doing nothing day after day. There was only one thing left for him to do. After school he almost ran outside and when he saw the boy he went up to him.

"Well, Ernest. Nice to meet you here," he said cheerfully. "I have to go on an errand close to where you live. Perhaps we can walk together."

The boy seemed to be pleased about the company, and they fell into an easy step as they talked quite informally, until they arrived in front of his house.

"Tell me," the teacher asked, "you live with your mother, don't you?"

The boy looked at him in surprise. "Yes," he said.

"Why, perhaps you would not mind if I waited for her. Because of the personnel form for the office. You know, we never got it, and the people in the office have already asked me several times. Won't she be home soon from the hospital?"

"From the hospital? Is she sick?" the boy was obviously concerned.

Ernest blushed. Obviously he had made a huge mistake. "No, no," he said hastily. "I thought she works in the hospital. I'm sorry, I didn't mean to worry you."

"She works in a department store, and she is home now," the boy informed him. "I imagine it's all right if you want to come up. Today is her afternoon off."

So he had done that to her too. He had ruined her career and now she had to go and sell blouses in a store. He began to tremble slightly and wondered whether he could even face her.

"Well, if you think she wouldn't mind. The school really needs that form."

He breathed heavily as they walked up. The boy had a key so they could walk right in. Just one more door...

"Mom!" Ernest called, "Mom, Mr. Batcher is here."

"Who?" Was that her voice? He tried to remember. "Oh, yes, your teacher, of course. I'll be right there. Ask him to sit down."

Two minutes seemed like a century, and when the door opened, a strange woman stood in front of him.

"You are Martha... I mean...forgive me, I just wanted..." He could not finish the sentence.

She rescued him. "Why, Mr. Batcher," she said kindly. "I believe you are still out of breath from those stairs. They are quite awful. I had to get used to them too when we first moved here."

Ernest lamely excused himself once more. He was ever so grateful to her. Then he explained the reason why he had come up to disturb her free afternoon.

"Heavens, yes. Those forms. I keep forgetting them. There are so many papers to take care of when you move, I'm sure you know." He assured her that he understood perfectly and was quite agreeable when she offered to make him a cup of coffee while she would fill out the information right there.

When he was about to leave she held him back at the door for a moment. "You've taken me to be someone else, haven't you?" she asked. All he could do was to swallow hard and nod in agreement.

"Probably my sister-in-law," she said. "Her name is Martha, and I think you have studied at the same university." When he said nothing, she added, "Were you friends?"

"More than that," he admitted. He simply could not lie about that. "Do you know where she is?" he asked.

"I've never known her," she answered. "When I married her brother, she was already gone, and then later when my husband died I lost track of the whole family. It's not always easy with a young child that needs all your attention."

Ernest only nodded. Was he relieved about the boy, this boy who had nothing to do with him?

"I think she's in Australia, yes, I am quite sure, somewhere in Australia," she went on.

Oh, my God, so far away, and in that huge country. Could she not tell him anything more definite?

She tried hard. "I think in Sidney. It was all so long ago. Yes, I'm quite certain now. In Sidney. In some hospital there. Does that help, do you think?"

Later he remembered that he had not even thanked her. He rushed down the steps and hailed a taxi. For all he cared they could haul his car away from where he had parked it near the school. What he needed was a telephone.

Not for one second did he think that there must be a difference in time between here and Australia. The long distance operator must have thought that she was dealing with a mad man. "A call to Sidney, Australia," he almost shouted. The name is Wolltin, Martha Wolltin. Try every hospital there." She assured him that she would try.

A carrier pigeon would have gotten there faster. Three times he urged the operator to hurry, and three times she assured him that she was doing her best. Then, finally, a ring. "I think we have her," she said. "Just a moment"

At the other end there were voices. English speaking voices that he could not understand. And then someone said, "Dr. Wilkin?" in a strange inflection. But that was enough, he knew that he had not ruined her career, and that she had succeeded far beyond her own expectations. And then he heard a voice that he would have recognized through centuries. "Martha!" he shouted. "Martha! ... Marry me!"

He was aware of some static in the line, but he knew that she had not hung up. "Oh, Martha, please," he said again, but much quieter now. "I've been such a fool. I beg you, sixteen years too late, but please marry me." Through the static he heard something. What was it? And then he knew. She was sobbing. But through all the static he felt that these were happy tears, and that she had said "Yes".

THE BRIDE

Once again they had quarreled, and that is why he now sat all by himself in his favorite bar. Well, that sort of thing happens when one is engaged, but normally only occasionally, and generally also with the same fiancé. In his case, however, this seemed to happen regularly, and with an entire collection of young ladies, all of whom had imagined that they were on the verge of marriage. To be fair, he had also thought so, quite honestly, and it was really too bad that the fault always lay with her, whoever she was at a given time.

He emptied his kirsch, a drink which up to now had always consoled him on occasions like this. In fact, it was his fourth glass already, because Becky had been extraordinarily beautiful. Even Barbara with her doe eyes had only cost him three. But he also noticed, that he was already beginning to think of her in the past tense. It was over and done with, she no longer existed for him; the crisis had been overcome.

Much relieved, he ordered a cup of coffee. Wonderful this feeling of health restored once more. The coffee came and life began to look cheery again, so that he was ready to stop thinking of his problems and to survey his surroundings like any unattached male sitting in a bar. Perhaps his future bride was already at the next table. But to do him justice, that is not what he thought. He was no rake, someone who was only interested in a one-night stand. In fact, he was thinking about the theatre tickets that were in his pocket for tonight's performance. Maybe he could still find a nice companion, a girl who would be pleased to have him save her from loneliness for the next few hours.

How about that little one over there? She seemed a bit young, of course, but that might be an advantage, because young girls don't yet have any firm opinions. It might avoid a quarrel about differences of opinions. She actually seemed to respond to his glances in her direction, and he was about to smile back at her, when he noticed that that response had not been meant for him, but for a young fellow who, beaming broadly, had just come through the door. Apparently she had been waiting for him.

"Well, she is really just a bit too young," he thought. "The reason one doesn't have a quarrel with children like that, in spite of her large blue eyes and those long lashes, is that one simply has nothing of interest to say to each other." After all, he was already thirty-four.

His glances continued to rove around the room, and this time remained fixed on a blond woman. Yes, more a woman than a girl, probably already in her middle thirties, with rather large black horn-rimmed glasses, but pretty just the same. No, pretty is actually the wrong word, because pretty demands a certain aura of warmth, and that did not seem to be part of that woman. Probably she was a career woman with that don't-touch-me frigidity. No doubt she was efficient, successful, a woman who probably made use of compliments to her own advantage. He would just make himself ridiculous with her.

When he had consumed his third cup of coffee, he realized that none of the candidates present were quite satisfactory. Certainly the intellectual-looking girl with the bad skin had very good looking legs, and that quite distinguished lady, probably in her forties, had lovely hands; and how about that rather masculine face on that woman with the wonderful figure?

He wondered: "Am I too hard to please?" In his mind he ran through the list of his girlfriends and brides during the past few years. Each one of them had had her little faults, external blemishes, which initially he had accepted, and which had in the end not been responsible for the break up. "Rather an intellectual matter," he thought, not without some pride. "No, I am not really too demanding, too choosy," he concluded. "So what was it about these women that they had not been able to appreciate him properly?" He was quite certain that he was deserving of this appreciation.

"I am not a difficult person!" Without wanting to, he had said these words out loud, quite loud in fact, as if they would gain credence by his volume. Heads turned in his direction, and as rapidly as possible he paid his bill and fled the scene, which inadvertently had become a public confessional.

It took some time, not weeks, but days, until his normal equilibrium returned. He convinced himself that he should not give up the search, full of disappointments as it might be. It would all be worth it once he had found the right girl. Carried by this insight he returned to his favorite bar, talked to a pretty blond thing who sold ladies' stockings in a department store, went to the movies with her, to the beach, danced, and two weeks later replaced her with an unemployed waitress. Only once during that time a somewhat extended relationship developed, which lasted for almost four weeks. This one with a young French student who spoke almost no English.

As matters developed, she had just announced in French in words and in manner that were impossible to misinterpret a firm "au revoir", when fate opened an entirely new avenue for him: He found the woman of his life! Well, he did not really find her, but rather he invented her. Right in the midst of this torrent of foreign-sounding words, which he did not understand anyway, he suddenly remembered a sentence his mother had spoken to him a long time ago when he was only 20 years old. He had complained to her about his lack of luck with the girls in his college. What she had said was: "The way you are and what you want, you'll have to design your own model or just give up altogether until someone finds you."

At the time he had been rather hurt, but now, many years later, he wasn't so sure that there was not a lot of merit in the idea. He had, after all, gathered a good many experiences with women, enough to know that the perfect one simply did not exist, at least not in the real world. Nevertheless, each of his former fiancés had shown some characteristic or other that had warranted his approval. He could begin with that.

As a start he went to the dime store to buy a clean, new notebook. In the evening, in his customary bar, he settled quite unusually in a secluded corner without displaying the slightest interest in any of the unattached ladies. Almost as soon as he opened his notebook he realized that he would face problems. He had planned that on the very first page there would be her name. Now in no way should it be the name of one of the real girls he had known. That might influence his judgment and awaken memories he would just as soon forget. At long last he decided on Babette. It was a rather flirty sounding name (no, no, not because of that French girl) without being common. The danger here was, that some people might call her Betty, or even Babs, or perhaps Baby. Still, he liked the soft sound of the B's. He would just have to make it very clear to everyone when he was introduced her that she definitely wanted to be called Babette, and nothing else. (Yes, the 'e' was to remain silent.) Her family name seemed to him to be less important since she would, after all, soon have his own name.

With a firm hand he therefore wrote in the center of the first page: BA-
BETTE BECK.

Just having created the name filled him with enormous satisfaction,
enough to last him not only for the rest of the evening, but also for the entire
next day. However, just before he went to sleep that evening he softly whispered into his pillow: "Good night, Babette."

During the following week he divided his notebook into three parts. First
came merely statistics, those anatomical features that were generally indicated
by numbers. Since Babette was a perfectly proportioned being, it took him
some time to arrive at a harmony of resulting calculations. Much to his surprise, the time spent on the determination of the individual physical attributes
as expressed by numbers afforded him a great deal of satisfaction.

The second part was devoted to matters of general character traits. She
was cheerful and never crude. While she always laughed at his jokes, she
never tried to tell any herself, and looked shocked when someone else made
an off-color remark, although she was no prude. People would think of her
as charming, always well-mannered, and dressed stylishly without ever being
ostentatious. Naturally she was well educated, but she never flaunted her
education or tried to put him in the shadow when he expressed an opinion.
On the more practical side she was, of course, a very good cook, an excel-
lent housewife, frugal but imaginative in her taste when it came to deco-
rating her home. For our purposes let us just let matters rest here, it would
be too extensive a list to copy all the entries in this category. Suffice it to
say that she possessed every ideal trait that any normal man would list given
the same opportunity.

Perhaps we should also point out that he went about his work in a most
serious manner. Each characteristic was weighed in the balance for a considerable time, refined, honed to perfection, expressed in just the right manner.
For that reason he was really very proud of himself when he was finished with
the first two sections of his notebook; but just in case, he reserved a few additional pages for a rubric he called: possibilities of further development.

The third part then was to be a kind of diary of his life with Babette. Here
he reported about their excursions together, about visits to the theater, various
entertainments, her reactions to the news events of the day, her reactions to
his interpretation of those happenings, and many other matters. But not only
those matters, because with surprising sensitivity and discretion he described
their ever-deepening love for each other. Thus their first kiss stimulated an

excitement that he had never before experienced with any other girl. And finally, there was that enchanting, wonderful weekend in that quaint little inn at the lake.

Nothing could disturb this happy, idyllic existence. People who met him for the first time wondered why this young man would sit hour after hour with a blissful expression on his face. Most of them came to the conclusion that he was just a bit strange. Others, who had known him for some time, had been made aware of the existence of a very precious new girl in his life, though he continued to be very secretive about details, and none of his friends had yet met her.

In this fashion he lived on for slightly more than two years now, when suddenly she fell ill. Nothing really serious, but he worried just the same, especially when it seemed advisable that she should spend some time in the hospital. Immediately he himself felt so feverish and run down, that he had to call in sick for a few days. With increasing panic he thought of what life would be like if she would not recover. By phone he ordered a huge bouquet of roses from a flower shop, and had them sent to the hospital. Unfortunately the store reported upon inquiry that they had not been able to deliver them, since the hospital had informed them that no such patient had been admitted. With the strongest possible words, he entered his opinion about the obviously sloppy registration system in the hospital into his diary.

Then suddenly a frightening thought occurred to him. Since he had not actually defined her illness, it was even possible that her problem was not physical but psychological, or even mental. Had he been the cause of some sort of pressure, some sort of unforgivable emotional strain on her delicate soul? In a panic he jumped from his bed to his notebooks, in order to review once again every phase of their relationship. By this time he had already filled an entire library of notebooks, but there was nothing that pointed to any moments of unhappiness. It was a terrible time for him. How wonderful when she was finally released from the hospital, so that now he could himself find the strength to leave his own bed and his room for the first time in three weeks. Naturally she was unable to return to her normal life right away, since her doctor had recommended a period of three to four weeks to recover. Quite sensibly she had made arrangements to stay in an inn somewhere in the country where the air was fresh and life was very quiet.

When he himself appeared in public again, he was welcomed with considerable sympathy. People had had no idea that he had been so ill, rather everybody had assumed that he had been away on a honeymoon, and that they could now welcome his mysterious bride. He listened to these speculations with immense consternation. Naturally, he should have thought of it, this was the key to the inexplicable emotional sickness of his beloved. During all this time that she had shared his life, he had never once indicated by even the slightest hint that he wanted her to become his wife. Ever since they had met, he had felt so much that she was part of his life, that he wanted her to bear his name and his children, so he had forgotten about the legalities. After all, in the innermost part of his being he was a thoroughly conventional man, one who longed for home, for family, for security.

Immediately he sat down to write a long letter to her. Once again he recalled the wonderful times they had spent together, once again he declared his undying love for her, and in this manner his passion for her grew to the point where he asked her, nay begged her, that she would come to release him from his guilt. In short, he swore that as soon as she would find her way to him, he would immediately undertake the necessary steps toward a marriage.

When he had thus finished and poured out his heart, he felt immense relief. Carefully he wrote her name on the envelope in large printed letters and added the name of an inn in a resort town in Arizona that he had found in his AAA book. Just to make sure, he added, "Please forward". When he took the letter to the post office the next day, it required extra postage because of extra weight. What he now felt, however, was indescribable relief.

Since the clerk in the post office had insisted on a return address, the letter came back two weeks later. Actually he was quite surprised, but obviously she had gone to a somewhat cooler climate, and so he readdressed it to a location in Maine. Unfortunately, it seemed necessary to repeat this process several more times, until he had quite exhausted his knowledge of inns and spas. Upon the advice of a helpful girl in a travel agency, his letter next made the round of all Holiday Inns, Days Inns, etc. All in vain, although he now began to receive a mass of catalogues and brochures from attractive sounding resorts all over the country. One can understand, that he soon completely lost his enthusiasm as time went on, and it was some time since he had last written into his diary. In fact, matters had reached a point where he even occasionally discussed this or that attractive brochure with one or the other young lady of his acquaintance.

That was why he was completely unprepared for what happened next. Among the letters he normally received from the various hotels, there was one that did not contain another prospectus, but a handwritten letter. "My beloved Bunny" was written on top, the very pet name that Babette had often playfully used to call him. "I knew it," the text went on, "I have always believed that we would find each other. Heaven only knows how often I have written to you, and told you that I am well again, and that I love you more than anyone else in the entire world. How I cried when I learned that the hospital had returned those surely exquisite roses you so thoughtfully sent me. How dumb of us that from the very first day that we met we always used our special names for each other, so that I never even knew your last name or where you lived. How lucky that from the beginning I had written everything into my diary. Now I set out to reread everything (what wonderful times we had) to find a clue where I might reach you. I can't even count the number of letters I wrote that were always returned to me. But now your name and your address is no longer important, because soon it will also be mine, and I will never again forget it. Enough words, my lover, I must pack and hasten to be with you." The letter was signed with a little heart and the name Babette.

Scarcely had he read the letter for a second time, when he heard the doorbell. Quickly he ran his comb through his hair and adjusted his tie. Then he opened the door for the girl who with a radiant expression fell into his arms.

A VISIT TO A LITTLE TOWN

It was now four years since Fred Lyon had become a widower. So much had changed in his life since Rose had died. But, of course, that was to be expected when two people had lived together for almost forty years, forty happy years it should be noted. At first, life had not seemed quite so lonely. He still had his business, and his many friends had made it a point to invite him often enough to make him feel less abandoned. While he was grateful for their concern, he wished that a number of them would abandon their obvious efforts to see to it that he would meet a number of very nice and eligible widows. Also the children who lived at the other end of the country seemed to make it their duty to telephone and even to come and visit him more often now, so that all in all he was at the point where he even cherished the occasional evenings he could spend at home quietly by himself.

But now enough time seemed to have passed that those kindly efforts made by all to help him over his loss no longer were on everyone's mind. In addition, he had sold his business, which had also consumed a good portion of his time and energy all of his life, so that he was quite officially retired. To his surprise and his pleasure, he discovered that he actually relished this time of greater leisure. Far from being bored, he had begun to read books he had always put aside for a later time; he went to concerts, and he even considered taking some courses at the university. But frequently he also simply sat back and just idly let his thoughts run on. Understandably, it was inevitable that he would reflect back on his own life, on times of struggles and times of joy, and about the plans that he and Rose had made for the time when he would be free to come and go as he wished. But now these things were not to be, because she was gone.

One of those plans had involved a trip to Europe, back to the place where he had been born and which he had had to leave so abruptly under such unpleasant and unexpected circumstances. There had been years when he was sure he would never want to go back there to that place from which so much hatred had driven him and which had cost the life of his parents. Yet, that time also lay far behind him now. He had always known that he would never forget, but he had rarely given thought as to whether he could or indeed should forgive. He remembered how appalled he was when his son suddenly showed up as the owner of a used red Volkswagen. Couldn't he have bought some other car that was not German? But then, very soon some of his friends began to drive a Mercedes, "because they are such great cars and such a good trade-in". But those matters had only occupied fleeting moments in the past. He had grown to be quite satisfied with his own life and was thoroughly comfortable as an American. Besides, he was certain that he did not really have the time or to desire to go back there. He now remembered that when he and Rosa had casually talked about it, she had occasionally urged him to make time, because she believed it would be good for him to deal with what for him was obviously still a ghost from his past. "We'll go when I'm retired," he had always said, but even at the time he was never certain he meant it.

But now he was retired, now he had the time and there was nothing to keep him back, except perhaps his own reluctance. Rose had been right, he thought, he should go there and see the place and try to recapture the moment when his life had unexpectedly turned in a completely unforeseen direction. Suddenly, it seemed, this train of thought had become more than the mere pursuit of a casual curiosity, it had become a necessity, indeed a compulsion. He had to find out about himself; he felt that by going there now he would close a circle.

It was easy enough to complete the necessary arrangements, and within a matter of just a couple of weeks he found himself on a plane to Frankfurt. How quickly a plane could take him there. He tried to remember how he had felt when he had left Germany, 18 years old, with only ten German marks in his pocket, because that was all he had been allowed to carry with him. He had been fortunate enough to have an aunt in Portugal who had agreed to take him in temporarily until he could find a country that would allow him to stay permanently. Seen from today, that seemed a ludicrous problem, now when the world was open to young people from wherever they came. But in 1938 no nation was anxious to welcome a young Jewish boy from Germany.

They all had their own problems: depressions, unemployment, and quite generally anti-Semitism even in spite of the globally expressed abhorrence of the official hatred and persecution in Germany.

Of course, at that time he had not seen all of that clearly, and yet there was a great sense of relief of having escaped a fate that was ever more certain to lead to his internment in one of those camps that for several more years the world was unwilling to believe in. Although so many doors were yet closed to him, he had no fear of the future. In fact, there was rather a sense of excitement, of expectation, of curiosity as to what might happen next. Where might he land eventually? What would he be doing ten years from now? So many questions that needed answers, but at no time had he been filled with fear. He was, after all, only 18 years old, and seen from that perspective the entire matter was rather an adventure.

The landing in Frankfurt went smoothly, and the huge airport, which efficiently channeled passengers along their proper path, impressed him immensely. He hardly felt as though he had landed on German soil since so many signs and announcements could be seen and heard in English and in an entire variety of languages. Kennedy Airport seemed primitive and provincial in comparison.

His travel agent had made arrangements for a reservation in a hotel in Frankfurt for the first night. Here too everything was spotless and new. Of course, so much had been destroyed in this city during the war, he remembered pictures he had seen at the time. But now, everything that had once been typical and even quaint in this large city had disappeared and been replaced by a modern architecture that you could find anywhere in the world today. 'Uncultured' was a term that popped into his mind as he rode through town in a taxi. Maybe he would stay one more day just to take a closer look.

After a lengthy nap, he decided to eat his dinner in the hotel. The large dining room was also filled with foreign voices and foreign faces. Large numbers of Orientals seemed to be everywhere. As soon as he sat down, the waiter handed him a menu in English, and asked him whether he might have a drink in the same language, although he had not said a word to indicate that he was not German. In fact, it occurred to him that he himself had not yet spoken a word in his native language.

Fred spent the next day adjusting to the change in time, and with the help of a map looked for some of the historic sights of the city, which he had last seen in 1934. The old city hall, the Romer, was still there, or rather it was there again, since it had been restored after the war. Here too was the church in which Holy Roman Emperors had been crowned since 1562, and the St. Paul's church where the first National Assembly had attempted to forge a liberal united Germany and had failed. And then, finally, the home of the nation's towering classical poet, playwright, novelist and scientist Goethe which, he knew, had been rebuilt with contributions from all over the world. Fred remembered that in school they had had to read and memorize so many of his works which had been presented to them by teachers who had venerated this man almost like a god. As Fred looked around this thriving and hard-driving modern city, he wondered whether students today even had the least acquaintance or interest in these witnesses from a calmer, more romantic time.

On the next morning he made arrangements for a rental car. He thought he would enjoy the idea of driving a Mercedes through Germany. He remembered those cars from the time when he was just a boy, and how he had admired them when the great Caracalla won race after race in these supercharged machines. By driving one of them now, he somehow seemed to prove to himself that he had done all right.

Since this was to be a sentimental journey, he had consulted a rather detailed map, which would make it possible for him to stay away from the Autobahns and any other really major highway. He wanted to see the country unspoiled, untouched by the speed that was obviously on every German's mind when he hit his crowded highways. That seemed to be especially true when driving the Autobahn where it seemed to be Verboten to let any other car pass you.

'What a beautiful country,' he thought as he drove along in a rather leisurely fashion. The landscape with its gentle hills, its picturesque villages seemed so peaceful. It was hard to imagine that this was a place where such horrible things had happened to so many of his religious faith as well as to his parents and some of his more distant relatives who had not been able to escape. But he must not think of that now, to live in the present was a better beginning. Besides, were not most of the people he saw in passing too young to have been there or even to have been part of it? Still, one could not avoid the question what they knew about it now and what they thought about it in retrospect.

Quite unexpectedly his heart began to pound when he came to the first traffic sign that indicated the number of kilometers to his destination. He slowed down even more and eventually stopped at a convenient place. He'd been here before, right here. Was this not a place where he had been when his school had gone out to the country for a day of nature study? Had his teacher pointed out these very trees? Talked about the names of those distant hills? Fred could not remember them now, but it hardly mattered. He had lived in New York for so long and in all of those years it had never occurred to him that he might miss this sort of serene landscape. But now, just now, he felt such a strong sense of kinship as if something that had always been part of him had suddenly awakened.

Almost automatically he drove into town. By instinct or by deep memory he knew the way. The war had not been too hard on his hometown, no bombings had destroyed buildings, and no violent battles had devastated the heart of the city as had been the fate of so many others. In fact, everything looked the same but newer, fresher than he had remembered it. Obviously the town was prosperous and yet had maintained some of its former quaint characteristics. The timbered houses around the main square were still there, and there were even some young people sitting on the edge of the fountain as though they had been sitting there ever since he had left.

He had planned to stay in the Hotel Post, just off the center of town. He knew that there were newer more modern hotels available that were probably more comfortable. But that was not what he wanted at this time. He remembered the Post, really an old inn rather than a hotel, because here his father had met with some other businessmen every Wednesday evening to play cards, and occasionally they had gone there on a Sunday to eat with some friends of the family. In those days it had seemed to him to be a rather exciting place. For him, at least, going out meant going to the Post.

He felt strangely nervous when he parked his car in front of the entrance, but of course that was silly. When he walked in he immediately became aware of the fact that here nothing had changed. The tables were where they had always been; the large round corner table still had a sign that indicated that it was reserved for their permanent patrons. Even the pictures on the walls showing hunting scenes and the various antlers of stuffed animals shot by more than a generation of hunters were still the main decoration.

The voice of the innkeeper awakened him from his musings.

"Are you looking for someone?" he asked.

"Oh, no", Fred answered, "I just wondered whether you might have a room for me?" He suddenly became aware of the fact that this was actually the first time that he was speaking German since he had come to Germany. He wondered how much of an accent he had after all of these years.

The innkeeper looked just a bit surprised. Was it this request or his American accent?

"Well, yes, we do have rooms here," he said. "But you know, we are not really a hotel with Television and all that."

"That's not important, as long as you have a room, if at all possible with a bath," Fred assured him.

"It's got a shower. Maybe you want to look at it."

"That's a good idea," Fred agreed, and so they went up the stairs alongside the bar to the first floor. The room was at the end of the hall, quite large, just as he had expected it would be with scrubbed wooden floors, a very large bed, a night table, a couple of rather comfortable looking chairs, a massive dresser and even a desk. The three windows set in 144 patterns looked out the back into quite a good-sized garden. "That's just fine," Fred declared, "I'll take it." He did not even ask the price.

When they went downstairs again, he had to register in a big old book of names that obviously went back a good many years. He was tempted to search for familiar names, but then thought the better of it. When he wrote Fred Lyon and his New York address, the innkeeper merely commented, "I thought you might be from America. We don't get many guests from there; of course, just occasionally, an American soldier with a lady who he says is his wife. We don't ask. Times have changed."

Fred agreed but did not want to discuss the matter any further at this time.

"How long are you planning to stay?"

"I don't really know. Does it matter? Is the room reserved?"

"No, no, not at all. I just wondered. By the way, my name is Hans Bauer, I'm the owner."

"Yes, I thought so," Fred answered but let the man wonder why that was so. "Perhaps you have someone who can help me carry the luggage upstairs, and also you might have a better place for me to leave my car rather than on the street."

"Sure, you can drive it in back of the house, and I'll help you with the luggage. And, by the way, if you want breakfast in the morning, we can bring that to your room."

Fred agreed that that was just fine.

When he was finally alone in his room, he immediately set out to empty his suitcases, hang up his clothes, and put things in the dresser and in the bathroom. He smiled just a bit to himself. "I'm making a nest,' he thought 'as though I am settling in here'. Suddenly he felt just a bit weary. Was it the drive? Or was it the onrush of emotions that had seized him about being here after all of those years. He opened the windows wide and settled for just a moment in one of the chairs. Not surprisingly, he fell asleep.

When he finally woke up again, dusk had begun to fall and there was a chill in the air. He closed the windows. Actually he had wanted to take a stroll through the town and then have dinner in one of the restaurants he might remember. But that could wait now; he would start his walk down memory lane tomorrow, when he was fresh and rested. After all, he could eat here just as well.

After he had freshened up just a bit, he went downstairs where he found much to his surprise that the place was quite crowded. How good, that none of the chatter had penetrated up to his room.

Hans Bauer seemed pleased that he had obviously chosen to eat here, and ushered him to an empty table from where he could observe much of the rest of the room. When the waitress came, he ordered a glass of Dortmund beer. Not because he remembered it from former days, when he could not remember ever having had a beer, but because of a poster over the bar. Happily, he found it to be very good. The moment when he studied the menu he immediately knew what he wanted, and this time it was because of memories,

And so he ordered the beef roulade with red cabbage. When it came, it tasted just as he had remembered and he immediately decided that this would not be the last time he had ordered it.

Only now did he become aware of the fact that he must have been hungrier than he had realized, for his entire attention had obviously been concentrated on his food. But now, for the moment, a feeling of great contentment seemed to have seized him. "Yes" he told the waitress when she inquired, he would have another glass of beer, and then he settled back comfortably to pay some attention to his surroundings. It was a somewhat mixed crowd there. A few tables with groups of men, some of whom seemed to arguing about something, while there were others who were giving evidence of having reached their limit of consumption of beer and schnapps by their reddened faces and their often loud laughter. In one of the corners several tables had been pushed together by a good-sized group of rather swarthy looking men who were obviously speaking in a foreign language. Probably Turkish, Fred assumed. And then, of course, there were those at the table marked "Stammgnaste" for the regular customers who were much engrossed in their card game.

He now remembered how proud his father had been when he was invited to join a group of businessmen at this very table who met here every Wednesday to play Skat, that traditional German card game. He wondered whether the same rules still prevailed that had dominated the social composition of such gatherings at the time. There were those groups made up of people with university degrees, doctors, clergymen, professors, and even the occasional pharmacist. Then the ones who worked for the various agencies of the government, civil servants, in other words; and finally, of course, the businessmen. None of these groups would ever mix up the social classification of their memberships. When he thought about it now, as an American who had socialized with all sorts of people, he found these arrangements exceedingly silly. Class consciousness was not something he had taken with his baggage from Europe.

Perhaps nowadays it was not even quite as rigid, you can't tell any more, since over here, too, people had begun to dress in the same casual style as in America. Anyway, he did remember how pleased his father had been at the time, because it had indicated to him that he had been accepted even though he was a Jew. Of course, all of that had changed in 1933 when it was made clear to him that his presence made the others in the group uncomfortable, until soon a sign appeared on the door that Jews were not welcome in this establishment.

Suddenly the memory of that time overwhelmed him. Yes, for a short time his family had been accepted, approved of by some of the same people who later stood by when their store was demolished by brown-shirted hoodlums, who now avoided his mother when she went shopping, and who had not voiced a single protest when his parents together with the other few remaining Jewish residents of the town had been loaded on trucks and carted away, never to be seen again. Had all of those former friends really believed that they would merely be resettled in the East?

Fred had buried all of those reminiscences for many years now. Of course, he himself had no longer been here, and all he knew about it he had learned after it was all over from that lady lawyer he had hired after the war to represent him in his claim for restitution. The new German government had finally settled the claim, and in this manner his "inheritance". The death of his parents in one of the camps, had helped him to start his own business in America. But now, here in this place, it all stood before him with such horrible clarity. He could not remember when last he had cried. Without paying his bill or returning the innkeeper's "good-night" he almost ran upstairs to his room.

Much to his surprise he slept very well and did not even dream. The garden under his window looked so inviting in the sunshine this morning that when someone knocked at his door with his breakfast, he asked whether he might be able to eat it outside.

"Of course you can," a female voice answered. "I'll set the table for you."

When he came downstairs, he found that a table had been set for him with a red-checked tablecloth under a large shade tree. A very pleasant looking woman was waiting for him and announced that she was Else Bauer, wife of the innkeeper, and that she hoped that he had slept well.

"Yes, indeed, I did," he assured her. For a moment he hesitated whether he should go on. In former days there had always been a respectful distance between a guest and the serving personnel. But, after all, he was an American, and there no such distance existed. Besides, she was, after all, the lady of the house.

"You have such a nice place here," he continued," and it seems to be so well run."

Her radiant smile was her thanks for the compliment. "How long have you owned this place?"

"Why, we have had it for seventeen years now. But before that it belonged to my father-in-law and even his father and grandfather before that".

"That's a wonderful tradition" Fred said.

"Yes, it is," she agreed, "and a great responsibility. Our son is doing his military obligation, but we hope that he will want to carry on when he comes back".

"Surely he will want to," Fred commented.

"Yes, we hope so. But nowadays things are different. Young people don't seem to think that tradition is so important. Isn't that so in America also?" she asked.

"Well, yes," he had to agree, "but in America we never think so much about tradition. Somehow every generation seems to think that their children ought to get some steps ahead of their parents. I never know really whether that is good or bad". Fred suddenly became aware of the fact that they were having a real conversation, more than just an exchange of friendly chit-chat. "Won't you sit down, Frau Bauer," he invited her. "I am actually getting quite a stiff neck looking up while I sit and you stand."

She blushed just a bit. "Why, thank you, Mr. Lyon," she said. "I didn't really mean to intrude, but it's so interesting to talk to someone who comes from so far away and can speak German." She pulled up a chair and seated herself somewhat primly on the edge of it. "I really hope you don't mind for just a moment."

"Not at all," he assured her, "and by the way, these rolls are wonderful. Now that is something we don't get in America, such nice crisp rolls".

"You've been here before" she guessed, "haven't you?"

"Yes, I have," Fred admitted. "In fact, I used to live in this town a long time ago." There, he had said it.

"We thought you might have," she admitted, "but you must have had a different name then. I mean, yours doesn't sound like a local name," and then she blushed again. "I'm sorry," she added hastily, "I shouldn't have asked that".

"No, no, it's really all right," Fred assured her. "People in America have a hard time pronouncing my German name correctly. That's why I changed it." He smiled just a bit. "I wasn't ashamed of it or hiding from the police," he said and he smiled. "When I lived here my name was Fritz Lowe; Lyon is simply a translation of it". And then he wondered whether he needed to do so, he added, "I left here early in 1939."

There was quite a long pause while Else Bauer kept looking at the ground. Obviously she did not know what to say next, and he liked her for it. So often people from Germany were likely to say, "You were lucky to get away then," and what they meant was 'you were lucky before the war broke out', but that was not why he had been lucky.

He decided to help her. "Of course that was long before you were born," he said softly.

When she looked up again he saw that there were tears in her eyes. "Yes," she said almost voiceless, "yes, it was. But I heard. It must have been terrible."

Fred merely nodded in agreement.

"You are Jewish, aren't you?" The very question seemed to embarrass her.

"Yes, I am."

"I hope it's alright to ask. I've never asked anybody this before. In fact, I'm sure I've never met anybody who is Jewish before," she added.

"Of course, it is all right. I'm not ashamed of being Jewish."

"Oh God, I didn't mean that. I really didn't".

Again he felt sympathy for her distress. "I know you didn't," he assured her. "Aren't there any Jewish people left here?"

"Yes, just a few I think. I'm afraid I have never met any of them. But I know there is a small synagogue. You must ask my husband, he knows a lot more about it. And maybe he'll also tell you about his father". Suddenly she seemed to be in a hurry and got up. "I really have to go now, but I was very..."

she was obviously groping for the right word, "very grateful that you talked like this to me."

'Was that the right word? Grateful?' But then he decided not to dwell on it.

When he had finished his breakfast, he knew that now it was time to do what he had come to do, to close the circle of his life that had begun in his place. Strange that it should be so hard after all these years. But instead of turning to the right when he left the inn, to the right where his parent's shop had been, where he had played on the street as a little boy, he turned to the left. Of course, he knew that part of town too, but it had not really been that much of a part of his early life. Friends had lived there that he had visited, some of them even after 1933 when having Jewish playmates had suddenly made some people say that you were unpatriotic. He particularly remembered Horst Lehmann who had been his best friend, but whose father had suddenly become an eager and important Nazi and whose son therefore had to join that youth organization that would educate him toward later leadership. Horst would suddenly walk past him in school as though he had never met him. Most likely he had joyfully gone to war and was probably dead by now. For just a few moments Fred wondered just how he would act and what he would do if he happened to run into him now.

Quickly he decided there was no point in dwelling on it. There had, after all, been others, Franz Kleinert, Helmut Braun, and some whose names he no longer remembered. In fact, he had to admit that he personally had not suffered all that much during those first years after 1933. Yet, increasingly, his teachers had obviously begun to put more distance between themselves and Fritz Lowe, who up to this time had been a promising student in their eyes. Before all of this happened, they had had every reason to expect that this pupil would go to the university and might well some day wind up on the honors list of their school. But, of course, people like that were no longer allowed entrance to universities, which, on the whole, they believed was really quite all right. Perhaps not, they felt, in the case of Fritz Lowe who was really quite a nice boy, and they felt very noble and broadminded as they thought so. Really, they did not mistreat him in any demonstrative way; they rather generally mostly ignored him when he raised his hand to indicate that he knew an answer. Most likely all of those teachers would be dead now, so that he could no longer ask them how they felt about all of this now.

Aimlessly he wandered on, stopping for seconds in front of one or the other houses where he knew he had been to visit a friend for a birthday party or to do schoolwork together. But he rejected the idea that he might stop to inquire about the family. What was the use? And did he really care about them after all of this time? Maybe he should change direction and walk to the business district where he might find a cafe and stop for lunch.

What had been the main street was still the obvious shopping district, but now it was a walking street. Fred approved of that idea. Here you did not have to dodge traffic as you have to in New York. People who wanted to window-shop could do so, and people who were in a hurry would use the center of the street. But, to his surprise, the shopping hours were still arranged more for the convenience of the store-owners than the customers. Stores closed at 5 in the afternoon, and some of them even had a two-hour lunch period, and all of them seemed to close early on Saturday afternoon. Well, it was, after all, a small town.

The department store was still in the same block, but the entire front had been modernized in a way that poorly harmonized with the rest of the old buildings. Naturally the former name, Oppenheimers, was now replaced by a name on a whole chain of stores that he had noticed everywhere else. Uncultured again! But just beyond the end of the street he saw another new building, also a modernized structure. On the marquee above the entrance he read "Alhambra". A movie house! A movie house that had once been the local synagogue. His family had never been very religious and their attendance at the services had been rather sporadic and casual. Of course, they had always gone for the various holy days, and he remembered his Bar Mitzvah and how proud he and his family had been then. More importantly, he remembered that ninth of November just before he had left this town forever when the building had gone up in flames and the Torah had been desecrated by a laughing brown-shirted mob. In spite of his emotions at the sight of this building he went over to it in the hope of finding some sort of inscription or plaque that would remind people of the original occupant of the site. His search was in vain. He had not actually seen the whole scene, because on the same day the window of his parent's store just down the street a couple of blocks had been smashed by a passing gang, and he had helped to clean up the mess. He remembered how his mother had cried, but also that his father had consoled her with the observation that some of the older people who passed seemed much embarrassed by the vandalism.

"You see," he had said, "they are the real Germans, and they won't allow this to go on much longer. Believe me, everything will be like before." Had he really believed that, Fred now wondered. The store itself still was there, but it now sold radios and TV sets.

So many thoughts, so many memories. It had been that very day that had determined his fate and, sadly, that of his family. His mother now had insisted, that plans that had only reluctantly been initiated be carried out. A distant relative in America had agreed to sponsor them if ever they could make up their minds to leave Germany. On that day she had insisted that at least her son must leave as quickly as possible and resigned herself to the fact that she would stay with her ever-optimistic husband. "They won't bother with us older people," he always said. Only two more letters had reached Fred in America, and when the war was over the German authorities had been able to inform him of the precise day and place of their death in the camps.

"I must get away from here," Fred thought as he felt some tears welling up in his eyes. Almost without knowing what he was doing he ran has hand over the stone wall as he caressed what had been and then walked away quickly and resolved never to come back to this part of the street again.

It was still too early for lunch, so he might as well see whether he could find another place on his unwritten list of remembrances. Yes, there it was, his old school, and looking quite clean and new. For a moment he hesitated, but then walked up the few steps to get a look at the inside. Obviously, classes were in session, and he could hear voices and even laughter. Had he ever heard laughter when he was at school here? As he remembered it, school was a place of repressed fear, fear of the unsmiling teachers, even of the seemingly all-powerful custodian who watched everyone from the moment you entered the building from a window right next to the entrance. Now everything looked much friendlier. There was a case with a collection of trophies and photographs from athletic events. Next to it a formal—looking plaque of remembrance with the names of the heroes who had once been students here and had "given their lives for the Fatherland in both World Wars."

"Are you looking for something?" someone interrupted his contemplation.

"Not really," Fred answered, "it's all right just to look around, isn't it?"

"Of course," came the answer. "Did you by chance go to school here?"

"Why, yes I did. Quite a long time ago. It seems so much lighter and friendlier now."

"One would hope so," the man answered, and then held out his hand and introduced himself. "I am Dr. Schiller, the principal here. We are always particularly glad to see former students here back for a visit."

"I am Fred Lyon," Fred took the other man's hand and as he said his name he could clearly see a quick reaction in the other man's eyes. Just to be friendly he added: " and when I was at school here, no offense, the principal and most of the teachers seemed to be quite old men."

Dr. Schiller laughed. "They certainly were. We have pictures from the old days. Those beards were quite impressive, although that may have been before your time."

"Some of them were like that, I do remember that."

"And now you are an American, I suppose?"

"Yes, I am now." Fred let the other work for more information.

"I see." There was a small pause. "And may I ask when you left Germany?"

"In 1939. In January".

"Oh, that was still before the war. You were lucky." Dr. Schiller immediately realized his mistake and blushed slightly.

"I'm sorry," he hastened to add. "I should have realized, of course. You are Jewish, aren't you?"

"Yes, I am".

"Those must have been terrible times," Dr. Schiller said slowly and in a soft voice. "Of course, I was not even born then so I only know what I have read. But everyone I know is very, very sorry about those matters."

They are sorry, Fred thought, but should they not be ashamed? Maybe that was asking too much, after all, to blame the children and to have them suffer for the sins of their fathers.

But then he said, "I see you have a plaque here of those who have given their lives in two wars. Did you ever think of having a plaque for the victims of those times? My father and three of my uncles also went to school here."

Dr. Schiller seemed embarrassed. "You are right," he admitted.

"We should have done that. We must never forget. Believe me, I promise you that I'll see to it, and when it's done we'll have a memorial dedication right here. Do you think you might come back for it?"

"Well, I don't know that. But you can write to me when it is done and perhaps even send me a picture."

"You can be sure I'll do that," he eagerly promised. "How many names would you think are involved?"

"I don't really know," Fred had to admit, "but surely you can find out. Germans are very good at keeping records. I am not even sure the numbers matter, even three were too many and should be enough to serve as a reminder."

"Of course, of course! But I'll still try to find out and perhaps we can even notify survivors that we have done this and invite them to visit. I think other German towns have done that and paid all the expenses for it."

Fred suppressed a slight grin as he saw how Dr. Schiller really get into the spirit of this mission. It was probably best not to ask about his real motivation.

"Tell me, Mr. Lyon." the principal went on, "could you stay until the classes break to meet some of the teachers? I'd especially think you would like to meet our Dr. Fell who teaches physics here."

"Why him particularly? I was not especially good in physics in school."

Dr. Schiller again seemed somewhat lost for words, but then confessed, "Well, I think he is partly Jewish. His mother, I believe, or his grandmother."

Fred just looked at him without any comment until the other hastily added, "you are right, it was probably not a good idea," and then he suddenly brightened. "I know, there is someone I know from your days at school here, Dr. Bender. She taught here too but now she is retired, of course."

"I don't know any Dr. Bender," Fred was puzzled about the other's suggestion.

"Of course, she was not Dr. Bender then. I believe it was something like Helen Feld or Weld. I'm sure you could find her in the phone book."

Helene! Helene Feld! Yes, he had not thought much about her since he had left, even though she had been his girl friend at that time. He was suddenly anxious to leave and be alone with his own thoughts. It was time anyway to thank Dr. Schiller for his good intentions and his courtesy, and to accept the other's regrets that he could not stay and perhaps even talk to one of the classes the next day. In truth they were both relieved that they had reached the point of parting.

For a time he just wandered around aimlessly until he found a cafe where he could settle down and have some lunch, but mostly where he could watch the world go by from his table on the sidewalk and devote himself to this new onrush of memories. Yes, Helene; She had been the first girl he had really kissed. In those days that was about as far as young people who thought they loved each other would go. Well, perhaps a bit more but not like today when they immediately went all the way. Yes, they had loved each other truly, and Helene had to endure some ugly remarks from others that she seemed to like this Jewboy, and she was not Jewish. It was almost illegal then, and she might easily have gotten in trouble with the authorities. She had cried when he had to leave, and he had assured her that he would send for her as soon as possible. He suddenly felt that he had left a debt unpaid. Once he had gotten to America, so many new experiences and problems had overwhelmed him that he never did get around even to write to her. Moreover, there soon was the war which had made a correspondence impossible.

Dr. Helene Bender! So she had studied, achieved a PhD and become a teacher. And, of course, she had married, just as he had married and she probably also had children. He wondered what her husband might have been liked and how she had managed through those years of war and the aftermath.

Back in his hotel he found a telephone book and while there were three listings for that name he was quite sure he had identified her. Should he call her? And what would he say after all this time? Still, he copied both her number and address on a piece of paper which he then carried around with him for the next two days while he wandered around aimlessly and somewhat restlessly. The street name meant nothing to him, and when he inquired of his landlord, he learned that it was in one of the new developments on the edge of town.

"At least I can look," he concluded as for the first time he retrieved his car from his parking place. Walterstrasse was not very far out of town. Nothing in this small town was, of course. It was a pleasant street, neat houses, none of them very large, but all of them with a bit of grass in front and obviously a small plot of land for a garden in back. There was a bit of sameness in all of these places, but Fred remembered that in Germany building permits had many restrictions to avoid the kind of helter-skelter developments you often found in America. There, number 38. He slowed his car almost to a crawl, but did not want to stop completely. People might wonder what he was up to. Someone, a man was working on some bushes in front of the house. Was that her husband? He could only see the man's back so that it was impossible to see whether it was an older man or not. Would he mind if Fred called his wife?

When he woke up the next morning he decided that all of this hesitation was really silly. After all, he was an old man, and she was of the same age, and there was probably nobody around any more who would remember them from the past. And even if… Still, his hand shook slightly when he dialed the number.

"Bender," a female voice answered. "Dr. Helene Bender?" he made certain.

"Yes," she answered but her voice sounded somewhat doubtful whether she should perhaps hang up.

"This is Fritz, Fritz Lowe," his own former name sounded strange to him after all these years, "perhaps you remember me."

"Fritz! Oh my goodness! After all these years. Of course I remember you. What a surprise to hear you."

The ice was broken and Fred knew that from now on talking to her would be easier. "I am here in town," he informed her, "and I thought perhaps we might meet somewhere for lunch and talk, if your husband does not mind."

"I no longer have a husband, Fritz," she informed him. So the man in the front yard had been a gardener or something, "He died almost fifteen years ago, and I'll be really glad to see you again. Why don't you...? No, it is probably better if we meet somewhere. Is your wife here with you? I assume you are married."

"No longer," he informed her. Rose died a few years ago now,"

"Oh, I am sorry," she said. What else could she have said? Then they arranged where and when they would meet for lunch and after she had hung up he sighed a deep sigh of relief. However, there was a new problem now. Would he recognize her after all this time? Besides, what would she think of him when she saw him again. He went into his bathroom and looked at himself in the mirror. Not too bad, he concluded, but then he made a face at himself to underline how silly he felt. After all, he was no longer a teenager getting ready for his first date.

He arrived at the restaurant ten minutes before the appointed hour, and found a table from which he could watch everyone who came in. He was quite certain that she was none of the women who came in and looked around. When she finally appeared in the door he knew her immediately. What a good looking woman she had become! Gray hair, of course, but still a good figure, and quite stylish looking. Fred even blushed a bit as he contemplated his own portliness.

Helen also had recognized him right away, and there was a large smile on her face as she came to his table. "Fritz," she said, as she held out her hand to him, and when he took it she withdrew it quickly and gave him a friendly hug. "You don't mind, do you?" she asked, "after all, we have known each other for a very long time."

Then they talked. There was so much that had happened in all of those intervening years. She had gone to the university after she had finished school, not so much because of a thirst for knowledge, but it seemed to her the safest place to avoid so much of the hysteria of the Nazi years. Of course, it had also affected the universities a great deal, but she had buried herself in studies and discovered she even enjoyed it. When it was all over she had quickly gotten a teaching job, since there was nothing in her record that indicated any political involvement during those past years. It was not long after that that she had become the principal of the school. Her brother had been killed in the war in Africa, and both her parents had passed away a short time later.

"And your husband?" Fred asked, but then wondered whether he should have asked.

"Actually, Paul and I met in a bookstore where he worked at the time. He had been wounded in the leg in the war and was very conscious of his limp. But he was a nice, gentle man who loved to read and who was just as alone as I was. We were really very happy with each other. It was, in fact, that war injury that eventually took his life."

"You have children, do you?"

"Yes," Helen answered, "we have two, one boy. Well, he is a man now, of course, but he lives in South America, a business man, and I don't get to see him much. My daughter, Paula, she lives in Bonn and works for the government and has been married a couple of times. In fact, can you believe it, I am a grandmother, even though I can hardly talk to my grandchildren who speak mostly Spanish."

Fred reached for her hand and held it in his. "We are well matched now," he smiled," I am a grandfather, although I can speak to my grandchildren, or rather, they can speak to me, and even though they are really quite grown up by now, most of their sentences seem to begin with 'I want'."

They spent almost all of their time together during the next few days. As often as not he would now spend the evening at her house where she would cook for him, and they would talk until almost early in the morning. Increasingly he became aware at how comfortable he felt with her. So many details had still to be shared. His days in the American army in the Pacific, how he had met his wife, how he had built up a very comfortable existence for both of them, what it was like to live in America and how proud he felt to be an American.

"It must be a wonderful feeling, that," she would muse.

"We in Germany unfortunately must carry too much unhappy baggage and shame from the past to feel that way."

Then they would talk about other places they had visited. His vacations in Florida, visits to California, wonderful times in Bermuda, and a cruise to Alaska, and those American wonders like the Grand Canyon. Helen had been in Italy and Yugoslavia at the beach, and had been much moved by a trip to Israel some years ago. Strange how often he had thought of going there himself because as a Jew he felt he ought to go, and she was the one who had actually been there.

"Can you believe it, there is one place I have always wanted to visit, even when I was a little boy, and that is Berlin. So many interesting and exciting things have happened there."

"Then why don't you go?" she suggested." It's not so very far from here."

"Would you go with me?" he asked in an almost breathless tone.

"Why not," she said. "I'd like that, and I have not been there for a long time myself. They have wonderful concerts and theaters and museums."

Two days later they were on their way. He drove his rented Mercedes while Helen studied the map to direct him. It was still early in the afternoon when they checked into the hotel Kempinsky. After lunch they walked arm in arm down the Kurfuerstendamm window-shopping, and whenever she admired something in the windows, he begged her to allow him to buy it for her. "I enjoy just to look,'" she assured him. "I don't want you to buy me anything."

In the evening they went to the symphony, and while he was no great connoisseur of music, he felt that this had been an extraordinary experience. Later, before returning to their hotel they stopped for a glass of wine at Mampe and watched the world promenade outside without saying very much.

It seemed a most natural thing that they were lying in bed next to each other at the end of this day. "I should have asked you, shouldn't I, before I registered us for one room?" he asked her.

Helene propped herself up on her elbow and looked fully at him. "Maybe you should have, but you already knew what I would have answered. Besides, I am actually rather flattered that you would want this," and then she bent fully over to him and kissed him for a long time. "You see," she smiled," we have joined the twentieth century at last."

He looked radiant when they appeared at breakfast the next morning. "So what will we do today?" he asked.

To his disappointment ,she answered, "I think we'll go home, Fred." He did not even notice that for the first time she called him by his American name. "Yes, I think it is better," she asserted.

It seemed to be a very long trip back, and neither of them said very much until they were almost home again.

Finally he broke the silence, "Helen; will you marry me? You must know that I love you."

"And we would live here in Germany?" she asked slowly.

That was a question he had not considered. "No, not really. I thought that you would come to America with me. You do speak English, don't you?"

"Yes, I do speak English, but that is not really the problem."

"Then what is?"

"We now know so much about each other's life during all those years when we were apart. I can understand why you would not want to live here again, and I hope you can understand that too many things have happened to me here that there are roots that hold me to this country."

Before he could think of a persuasive answer, they were in front of her house. After he had brought her baggage in, she put her arms around his shoulders. "I think we both have a great deal to think about, I believe. Perhaps it is best if you do not stay this evening," and then she kissed him and pressed him close to her.

When his landlady brought his breakfast the next morning after he had spent a most restless night, she also handed him a letter, which, she said, had been delivered for him early this morning. Instantly he knew what it would say, and for the longest time he just sat and stared at the envelope. When he finally opened it, it was just a brief note, "Dear Fred," he read, "do you remember telling me about your Rose, urging you to confront your ghost from the past, and of your compulsion to close a circle in your life? Little did either of you imagine that I too would feel that need, for neither of you even knew me or thought of me at that time. Now it is done, and you must believe me that I was and am truly happy that we have met again, and that our two circles have become closed in a most harmonious fashion. Yesterday evening I had a call from my daughter in Bonn that she would need me there. Maybe it is fate again, but it is probably best that it ends this way. I will always think of you and I am certain you will think of me, but do not try to reach me again. With much love," it was signed simply "Helene."

Almost three years later the mail brought him a quite official, looking letter from Germany inviting him to the dedication of a plaque in memory of the victims of the Third Reich in his former school. All of his expenses would be paid and the hope was that former students or their survivors would do them the honor to attend. The main speaker was to be a former principal, Dr. Helene Bender, who had chosen the theme: What Could Have Been and What Should Have Been."

After reading the invitation twice with a smile of satisfaction, Fred disposed of it in his wastepaper basket.

FOR MEN ONLY

But ladies may read it too, because they are mainly the problem of this report. That is, they are not personally the problem, but their birthday is. Can you imagine a man anywhere in the world for whom a birthday present for his wife is not the cause for many a sleepless night?

Strange, it does not appear to be that way the other way around. It seems that a wife always knows what her husband wishes or needs. I, for my part, accept this fact gratefully as something mysterious, and I am even inclined to surround it, with a somewhat mystical aura. But that is only a very personal view, because we live today in an age that rejects everything mystical as unsatisfying. Since science is the hallmark of this era, perhaps a scientist could look into the matter. It may just be possible that such research could lead to a biological discovery, which even in this day and age of unisex would demonstrate a very basic difference between the two sexes.

It may be of interest that I, myself, have already made a start. In a totally scientific manner I have inquired from 1843 men all over the world, just what they give their wives for their birthday. Also, I wanted to know how they arrived at the decision, and whether they were able to judge how their gift was received by the lady in question. For that reason I now want to thank all of those who have answered my postcard and herewith publish the results, so that the, public at large will be able to react, and may even use the product of my research as a guide for the future.

At the very first perusal of the resulting answers, it immediately became clear to me that any system concerning the solution of the "Wife - Present - Problematic" (henceforth to be addressed as WPP) must seek agreement with certain classifications of husbands. Thus, for example, I am in possession of 132 answers indicating that this problem was never solved personally by the male spouse, but became an assignment to a competent secretary. In fact, there is some reason to believe that the purchase of presents for family and friends (and occasionally girlfriends) at various times of the year constituted the major task for such employees. 73 of those fortunate husbands from the upper ranks of government, trade, and finance did not even have the slightest idea what these gifts had been. However, since they could never remember any complaints from home in this matter, they considered themselves totally satisfied. By the way, a few of them inquired of me whether perhaps on occasion I might send them a price list for an 4 carat bracelet, since they suspected that their secretaries might have arranged for a little extra income from those purchases. And finally, 12 reported that they had received my inquiry just at the moment when they had come home from the divorce court where their wives had charged them with neglect and estrangement, even though in the last five years they had received six vacuum cleaners, 72 pairs of kit gloves and 8 bread making machines for their various birthday and Christmas presents.

Before we leave these well-fixed gentlemen, two further cases also deserve our attention in the interest of our detailed and far reaching inquiry into WPP. An Italian playboy reported to us that he routinely inquired of his girlfriend of the moment (he changed them several times a year) what she would like as a present, and then used the information to purchase exactly that gift for his wife whom he had loved all along. As a result his wife now owned twelve mink coats, eleven thousand stock certificates in the Fiat Company, and a herd of beef cattle in Argentina. By the way, we were not told whether the girlfriends received the same gifts.

And finally, we found the solution to our problem suggested by an Arabian oil sheik most interesting. He reported that whenever one of the wives in his harem had a birthday, he granted as a present that he would be pleased to get rid of whatever rival she pointed out to him. He then saw to it that whichever one she designated would be executed immediately. This approach not only solved the WPP dilemma for him, but also gave him the opportunity to restock what he called his 'stable' with new blood.

Naturally conditions were quite different in good bourgeois circles. Most of all a very high percentage of those respondents admitted that they had not even attempted to deal with the WPP problem until the day before the birthday in question. Indeed after the third year of marriage it seems that a gentle wifely hint such as: "Perhaps we should go out to eat somewhere nice tomorrow evening, so that I won't have to bother with the dishes," is a favorite insurance formula employed by many a lady to make certain that her husband gets pointed toward a slight "Ah?...Oh!" direction, often somewhat puzzled whether the occasion is a birthday or an anniversary. It is then up to him to act as though he had planned for this moment all year long, while inwardly he is enormously grateful.

What follows then is a sleepless night for him, while in a sort of half stupor he wanders restlessly through an entire department store. The rules of the game now demand that upon rising in the morning he declares that it would be ever so much nicer to celebrate at their leisure, and that therefore he would wait until evening to give her his present. This is best done while he closes his closet door, or better yet locks his desk quite ostentatiously. Only very careless wives smile when they hear this little lie. They know! And as a matter of fact secretly they are aware that they have good reason to smile, because no one is as generous as a husband with a guilty conscience.

The actual purchase does not take very long and can easily be accomplished during the lunch hour (unless you have a secretary; see above). A necklace, a pair of earrings, a clip are the best selections, because they can be hidden in the pocket upon arrival at home. A mixer or a bread baking machine is obviously not a very practical solution for WPP under these circumstances. Now is the time to say "Oh, yes. Just a moment Dear," with a sort conspiratorial smile, go to the closet or desk and act as though you are rummaging around for a moment, and then triumphantly extract the nicely wrapped package (As an aside, I should also like to warn you that there are certain husbands who deliberately have left a small price tag on the underside of the box, so that she will truly appreciate how much she is worth to him. This is not nice!). It might also be worth reporting that a lady, who obviously censors her husband's mail, wrote on the margin: "The lady will do well if she is already dressed for the evening when her husband comes home, and all the appropriate jewelry for her outfit is already in place, otherwise it might happen to her that she must immediately wear those Christmas decorations set with red, and green glass.

Most husbands seem to know instinctively that for centuries now ladies have discouraged their husbands from buying something to wear for them. This is not necessarily a matter of wrong sizes or wrong colors. A locksmith from Ames, Iowa reported with great disappointment, that his wife has never yet worn that see-through blouse he had bought for her 58th birthday. To this day he cannot understand her reluctance. That young actress whose toilet he had unplugged looked so nice in it. In fact, now that he thinks of it, he even forgot later to send her a bill.

One of the worst things that can happen to a man is when he buys a gift that he has to wrap nicely himself. Which paper to select and then to fold it neatly around an object that is perhaps not totally square is bad enough. But then comes the decision: string or scotch tape? String is not very elegant, especially when it is a small present of an awkward shape. Scotch tape might be better, except that the damned tape is often hard to start because it is stuck so firmly to the roll, or you get it on the package all right, but it isn't straight, and you can't get it off again. And how the heck do those ladies make those nice bows? Whoever has gone through this agony once, is sure to buy something next year (earrings again) that gets wrapped in the store.

Amazing how unromantic so many men are. They buy brooms, pot holders (with cute patterns of cows or pigs on them), antique carpet beaters, tool sets. As a matter of fact, yes, many men buy things they themselves want, and somehow rationalize how much this will help the little woman: implements for washing the car, a lathe for his home workshop ("Just think of all the nice things I can make for you, Honey."), barbells ("I'll tell you what, I'll try this out, and if it helps me to lose some weight, we'll get a set for you too, and we can then do it together."). Then books: "Collected Football Statistics from the Turn of the Century to the Present." or even "'Historic Locomotives"(illustrated) You get the idea, I am sure, but be aware also that gifts of this sort are frequently listed as one of the reasons for divorce.

A problem allied to WPP is the matter of the obligatory card that must accompany any present. Funny? Sentimental? So that you can simply add your name to the text or even Blank. (Heavens!). Then there are those cards that fold out into veritable production numbers. And the texts!!! "While you're already sixty-seven, your kisses still send me to heaven!" Or humorous: "I must confess, you are a mess, but it's your birthday, so God bless." And then those when she is sick in the hospital: "Too bad you're sick, here my best wishes - Please get well soon, I'm sick of dishes."

I suppose you get the idea, so let us skip other examples. Money does not seem to be too successful. Mostly in the form of a check with a note "Buy something for yourself" lacks a great deal of warmth. Some men reported an incomprehensible lack of gratitude, even though the amount was as much as

$50. A Mr. V. in Texas believes that he has come up with the ideal solution. He has assured his wife that the real joy on a birthday comes from giving, and therefore he has convinced her that she should give him a present. This idea might deserve consideration, although here is not the place for it.

Planning is very important, and now we must point to Elmer F. from Chicago. Last year, on the day after his wife's birthday, he put a blank piece of paper in his wallet with the plan that whenever his wife would mention something she wishes she had, he would make a note of it, and then get it for her birthday when the time comes. Unfortunately he had to report that when he looked at that paper a week before this year's birthday all that was on it was "Jack Herlehy for lunch, 11:30". He couldn't even remember who that was, and he is quite sure his wife also didn't know any Jack Herlehy. As a P.S he added: "I bought her another pair of earrings." As you can tell by this time, earrings are very popular the world over, because they come in so many configurations, and are almost always appropriate. The only bad choice in this regard was reported by 18 Chinese gentlemen, who had purchased earrings engraved with the sayings of Mao that were now no longer in fashion.

Finally we must mention Shawn McCheap who reported to me the following,"....already as a very young man I knew that I would want to marry some day, but that the matter of her birthday would present a continuing expense. For that reason I searched far and wide until I finally met a young girl that had been deposited sometime soon after birth in a nunnery. The good sisters had found no indication of the girl's name or any information that would indicate her date and place of birth. For that reason I also cannot know her birthday, and we never can celebrate it. We have lived happily with each other for 43 years."

With these preliminary results of our study of WPP we express the hope that others will immediately exploit this subject matter in further serious research. The available wide area of sociological, psychological literary, historical and other allied fields, gives us the confidence to expect that before long universities will have organized a department for the major study of WPP. That leaves time for only one final request: "Will those 12 Eskimos who keep writing to me with the question "What is a birthday?" please cut it out."

LOVE LETTER
ON A MARBLE TOP TABLE

My Dearest:

Here I am sitting in a cafe in this city so far away from you. It is the same cafe and the same marble top table where we sat together, and laughed together, and were so happy together a long time ago.

Do you remember when I drew a small heart on this table with my pencil? It was meant for you but it is no longer here. Most likely this damned waiter who seemed so very nice at the time simply wiped it away with a damp napkin. Do you remember, Vienna seemed so romantic and charming then? Now it is cold and hard-hearted.

Weren't we alone in this cafe without anyone else? Now there are people everywhere and they want to crush me. And they are noisy and excited, a vicious crowd who seem always to be laughing about something or someone they all seem to know. Had they perhaps also talked about us, and even laughed about us? We simply did not notice it. But some seem so very serious as they read their newspapers and magazines. How can they? There is nothing in them about you!

More people...and some of them who are looking for a free chair look angrily at me. Am I sitting at their table? Impossible, this is OUR table. Do you think I might be able to buy it and bring it home with me? We could put it in the living room and in the evening drink our coffee there; and laugh; and be happy; very close to OUR table so that our knees will touch as they did then.

But isn't it possible that for those people with the angry look at one time OUR table was their table? Just as it was for us. - No, surely not. They just don't look like that kind of people. I can feel that quite clearly. At best they once closed a big deal at this table. But that doesn't give them the right to what belongs to us by the power of love. Business comes, business goes, but a love like ours is for always.

Do you suppose this table knows that sometimes it plays an important role in the life of its guests? Does it listen to what goes on? Does it perhaps even take part in it? I can see that there are a few numbers written down on the surface. What do you suppose they mean? The number for an account in the bank? Numbers for a lottery ticket? -No, I can see it quite clearly now, it is a telephone number. - Whose, do you suppose? Should I try it? That could clear up just one mystery in life. - No, I'd better not. In my present frame of mind it would be awful if it would be a garage or some office that answers. But it could be something else. A young girl wrote it. She sat here. All alone. Perhaps yesterday. Across from her a young man with whom she would have like to talk. Nothing dishonorable, she's not that kind of girl. But she was alone and would have liked some company. Too bad she had never learned to flirt but she noticed that the young man kept glancing in her direction, and he didn't have the courage to say the first word. And so she simply wrote down her telephone number on this table in the hope that he would notice it, and then she quickly paid and went home to wait for his call.

Might it be that she is still waiting? Does the table know that the young man never saw the number that might have changed his life? Is the number on the marble surface still faintly visible because the table hopes the young man will come back? Or that someone would call? Not I...someone for the young girl.

No, no, dearest, don't be afraid. I'll not call her. I am lonely myself and that would only depress her more. Especially when she learns that I have you and that I will soon return to you. And she has no one!

Of course, if that is all the way it is I must not buy the table and take it with me. Perhaps it will still find some nice young man for the girl, someone who will copy the number and call her and then loves her.

Anyway, telephoning is really a problem. I know because I tried to call you yesterday evening from my hotel. There you sit somewhere on a bed in an impersonal room with the receiver in your hand and wait, and wait, and wait. When we were here together the telephone was an enemy and our bed the harbor in which we wanted to lie undisturbed by the world. But now this wire was the only connection to you. You were too far away for me to hold you in my arms but this damned wire can do that. But I must try to caress you with my voice. –

A somewhat hoarse woman's voice said, "Yews, please?"

Impersonal, disinterested whether I should ask for your number or for some sort of office. Of course, I had to control my voice not to scream out my loneliness and my yearning. After all, that is none of her business. Still, we need her because without her and that wire I would have to drift like a rudderless ship on the ocean between us, without any hope of ever finding you. Only this pressing on buttons, plugs pushed in and then out, the mysterious secret language of the initiated, who know how to play this mechanical game can bring our voices to each other.

Then that hoarse voice came again, "Sorry, there is no line available at this moment. Do you want me to try again later?"

Nothing in her voice revealed the terrible judgment she had pronounced over me. I had sat down on the edge of my bed in the blessed expectation that it would only be moments that I can hear you. And now? Now I was banished to a lonely island like a prisoner. You exist somewhere in this world but there is no connection to you? Other things stood between us! Prices that have something to do with the stock markets; treasuries are discussing the values of foreign exchange values; reporters are dictating their reports from the war front; diplomats from all parts of the world are lying to each other in sweet tones. But for us, who love each other, there should not be an extra wire? Do you think if I turned to the United Nations they would be understanding of our dilemma?

Waiting is terrible. Some sort of sticky mass seems to hold back the hands on my watch. There is a mountain of cigarettes in my ashtray. You can't read in this frame of mind. — There, the bell after an eternity. "No, not yet". She has already tried it again after an hour. Perhaps in another hour. The message was delivered in a cold and impersonal manner. A real dragon this woman. - One hour! How short that can be and how endless this can be. The difference is wither you are part of it.

When we were finally connected it was too late. I knew it right away, but I could not make it clear to you because suddenly I had the feeling that the entire world was listening to us.

I could only hope that you felt what I wanted to say to you. That I love you! But I could no longer say it, there was too much standing between us.

Is it even possible to say this to a wire? I had the feeling during the entire time that this wire which was so inexplicable to me kept saying: 'Hurry; hang up; why do you waste my time with this nonsensical palaver? There are serious people waiting for me, people who want to talk about matters that are important to the world.

Then it suddenly came to me that our conversation did not really travel on the same wire, that we are not really connected to each other, even though the woman had said, "I'll connect you now!"

People nowadays just throw words like this thousands of miles into the heavens to some sort of giant gadget that floats around up there and then hurls my words to you back down to earth, precisely to the point were you are. Basically I don't mind throwing my love for you out into the universe, but only to the stars, to the moon, to the Milky Way, but not to a computer.

Can one even trust such a machine? You constantly read about "It's the computer" when something breaks down and you get the wrong bill. How can I be certain that my "I love you" is the same that reaches you? Perhaps some silly goose in California gets it, and you get the one from a bald-headed businessman who just now is lying in bed in Paris with a whore and automatically said it to his wife on the phone in Iowa so that she won't be suspicious. Does the Lord in heaven have a telephone? Does it help to pray?

That is why we only talked about trivial things. That is why I am not delivered from my loneliness and longing for you. That is why I am sitting at this table to look for you here. - But you are not here either. Only the number of that girl. Do you think one should call her?

Now I know how I can bring you here to me by magic. I'll just wipe out that number on the table with my handkerchief and with my pencil draw a new heart. I imagine that is also best for the girl. Who knows what sort of a person might telephone her. She'll be better off if she can look for a nice young man where she works or where she studies

....
....
....
....
.... I

was just about to sketch that heart when a lady sat down at our table. You know, they do that in Europe when there is no room anywhere else. She is quite elegant, probably in her middle thirties, reddish hair, very attractive. It seems she often sits at this table.

Of course, now I can't draw that heart, but she seemed to have noticed what I was about to do. "Just go on," she said to me and laughed in a rather charming way. Everybody else always writes on these marble tabletops. Yesterday I sat here with an elderly man, a foreigner most likely. He didn't know one words of German, but he wrote his phone number on the table.

He probably expected that I would call him.

....

....In a hurry

your
Freddy

ROLLO II

The beginning of it all was that we moved to the city. Not that we really lived in the country, but the area was rural enough so that we had no trouble keeping a dog.

This dog was my brother.

I am not just saying that, I really believed it. It seemed that quite by chance on the day that I was born he parked himself in front of our door and immediately made it clear to my parents that from now on they would have two new mouths to feed. So, as far as I was concerned Rollo was part of my life from the very first day that my mother carried me into our house. Of course, they knew where I had come from, but they were not at all sure how it had happened that Rollo had suddenly materialized. He was there; he seemed to care for me, which he demonstrated by keeping a constant eye on me, and so they accepted him as another member of the family.

Certainly Rollo was somewhat older that I was, although we were never quite certain about his age. At least he was housebroken, which nobody could say about me for quite some time. Still, speculation about his origin made many a meal in our house more interesting than it would have been without that subject.

Naturally Rollo was also there when I learned to crawl and quite often pushed me with his nose to encourage me, and lazy as I was I had great fun letting him slide me along the kitchen floor. Eventually I learned to walk, or rather, to run. I was too young then to realize that our age difference made it hard for Rollo to keep up with my energy. How he must have loved the hours I had to spend in school so that he could have a rest. Even now in retrospect I feel quite guilty about the fact that I had not always understood those pleading eyes, that tired wagging of his tail, even the occasional growling.

But then came the day when my father informed the family that we would have to move into town, the big city, and that he rather doubted that we could find an apartment where we could keep Rollo. I immediately hated him! Most likely he was not really my father! A stranger who had somehow inserted himself into the family! I informed him that I would simply keep my tent from the backyard and sleep in the park with Rollo. His assurance that he too loved Rollo left me cold.

My mother, who many years ago had studied psychology for three semesters tried a different approach. After all, she declared, Rollo was more or less a country dog who would be confused by all the traffic. Most likely he would end up miserably under the wheels of a car or a truck. Perhaps she should have taken some more courses in psychology because, after all that was not much of an argument. I, to, had grown up in the country and there seemed to be no question that they would take me along. Or was there? My counterproposal that I would stay where we were and they could come to visit us on weekends was also turned down.

It was a terrible time and Rollo who, of course, understood every word knew that the discussion was about his future fate. What was particularly depressing for him was the fact that he realized he was already of retirement age. And so, on the day when my father came back from the city where he had already been working for some time to announce that he had found an apartment for us, Rollo solved the problem - he died. Simply, quietly and gently.

For almost an entire month I did not speak a single word to my parents except for such phrases as: Capitalist Exploiters! Fascist Pigs! etc. I was fourteen at the time and had been enrolled in a very progressive private school were we heard a lot about modern sociology. Only when Rollo II arrived was harmony in our family restored to a more acceptable relationship.

I don't want to hide it from you; this Rollo was purple with white paws and a large red bow around his neck. My parents had won him as a prize at some sort of formal dance. Naturally, when they came home late that night I was already asleep, and so they placed him very gently at the foot end of my bed. I saw him instantly when I opened my eyes the next morning. Here he was, looking at me with these very large always inquisitive eyes as though he wanted to determine whether I was worthy of his attention. I stared back, at first in amazement and then hopefully. Surely this examination was just a matter of seconds but to me it seemed like an eternity. At last he gave a signal that he would try it with me. He wagged slightly with his tail.

Of course, you will now say that a stuffed dog can't wag his tail, that perhaps I only wiggled my toe a bit and imagined it all. I don't really care, for me he wagged his tail. And perhaps once also should not be so sentimental when one is fifteen, but I simply could no longer hold back my tears. "Rollo" I sobbed, "Rollo," and I pressed him against my heaving chest under the cover. I almost smothered him with my love.

For breakfast he and I, of course, appeared together, and for the first time since we had moved to the city I kissed my parents. However the greatest surprise seemed to be when I declared that I wanted to come along to the weekly battle in the supermarket. My mother inquired about this sudden interest so that I had to inform her that, of course, we would have to buy dog food for Rollo, and my sense of responsibility required that I would make the choice myself. My father seemed to want to say something that began with "but" when my mother quickly interrupted him and maintained that I was quite right and that we must not forget the dog. She seemed to have learned a great deal in the past months.

Naturally Rollo came along and did not seem to mind riding in a car. Unfortunately a sign told us that he was not allowed to come along into the store, but when I wanted to leave him together with some other dogs that had been tied up next to the store my father advised against it. He pointed out that after all Rollo was still very young and it was even possible that the other dogs had something against this sort of breed, since he was by no means just and ordinary every day dog. "Besides," he said, "if by chance he got loose from his leash he would never find his way home again." I agreed that he made sense and so Rollo stayed in the car, of course with the window slightly open. Perhaps you would also like to know that we bought dog food for $18 which we still have somewhere in the basement.

Well, on this first day my parents politely played along. They acted as though he was now being fed, put down a bowl with water for him, went for a small walk with him and me and the afternoon, and occasionally scratched his neck. Of course, he no longer wore that awful red bow with which he had arrived.

Unfortunately grown-ups have so little perseverance. When on the next morning immediately after breakfast I pointed out that we would now very quickly have to go out on the street with Rollo so that he could do his business, my father went on strike. To his own regret he announced that one must not go too for with certain matters, and the categorically forbade me to leave the house for this purpose. Revenge was not far off when he discovered a small pile right next to the front door and beside it an obviously distressed Rollo. What followed was a shouting match primarily directed toward me, although my parents should have known that I had been housebroken for some time. Nevertheless this demonstration fulfilled its purpose, and with a large sigh my father got dressed and we went for our doggy walk.

Does it surprise you to learn that soon Rollo became a real member of the family? My parents not only got used to him, they soon seemed to take him more seriously that they had Rollo I. Possibly I had done them an injustice at the time and they had really loved him. At any rate, there was no decision made in our house that did not take him into account. On the day that my father came home and told us that he had bought a real license for him, I knew that he now really accepted Rollo as a personality in his own right.

Unfortunately it was unavoidable that soon people in the house considered us to be mad, or at least wondered about our sanity since we could not hide it for long just what was going on in our apartment. In wind and weather we carried our dog into the street, once early in the morning and then again in the evening. When it was raining, we naturally carried him under our coat. Since we took turns those who got up early became quite used to the fact that one or the other of us would be standing by a tree urging Rollo to do his business.

Before we went on our summer vacation, my father wrote long letters to a number of hotels and motels to inquire whether they permitted dogs in their establishment. No wonder that when we checked in people though of us as jokesters but soon regarded us with concern since we naturally kept up our usual routine.

But then came that great day when Rollo finally proved to the world his true nature. It was the forenoon of a particularly dark and dismal day. I was at school, it was my last year, my father was in his office and my mother had gone shopping by herself. It seemed that Rollo had shown no interest in going along and seemed to prefer to rest on the couch.

Just then two men broke into our apartment. At first nobody in the house noticed it until suddenly everybody heard loud screaming on the staircase. One of the neighbors called the police and son the criminals were arrested within a block of our house. It had not been a difficult chase for the police since both men had considerable trouble running away because of their bleeding leg wounds. The doctor in the hospital later testified that they were the result of dog bites, and when the detective came to our apartment sometime later, he congratulated us on our attentive watchdog.

Since that time nobody in the house laughs about Rollo any more or about us. Indeed quite the opposite, whenever one or the other family plans to go somewhere for the weekend they ask us whether we could leave Rollo as a guard in their apartment.

INTERVIEW WITH MR. WOOF

Good evening Ladies and Gentlemen. Tonight we bring you an interview that we hope will help to clear up some of the questions many of us have about the threatening riots not only in our cities but also in our rural areas. An entire segment of our population has informed us that it is seeking recognition of its civil rights, and demands that immediate steps be taken toward a meaningful integration. It is therefore our hope that this interview will help to establish understanding rather than unleash further threatening unrest. It should also be said that we are most grateful to Chairman Woof who, we understand is dog tired from many hours of negotiations.

WE: We turn to you, Mr. Woof, because we believe that you, as chairman of your organization, are in the best position to explain the concerns that at this moment pursue your membership so doggedly.

MR.WOOF: You must understand, Sir, that any explanation that I can give here under these circumstances, represent only the very tip of an entire mountain of complaints, inadequacies, and prejudices. Our concerns entail, if I may put it this way, such a wide range of demands, that it is difficult to restrict them to just a single cause.

WE: Nevertheless, Mr. Woof, we would ask you to make clear some of your demands with precision, which surely is necessary if we are ever to clear the air between our kind and yours. MR.WOOF: Well,

I'll be glad to try. The operative term that can express our intent is "Co-Determination".

WE: You feel outvoted by your masters?

MR.WOOF: You see, here you probably quite unconsciously have touched upon a big problem. You said "by your masters", without considering even in the slightest that with these words you have expressed an attitude of a superior elite on the one hand vs. an inferior creature on the other. As so many of your kind you interpret your relationship to our kind as that of master and underling.

WE: And that is not so?

MR.WOOF: In no way is that so. Just consider, please, how our relationship comes about in the first place: A man, I am using this appellation quite consciously, because it can of course also be a woman, a person, if you wish, wants to enrich his or her life. (Parenthetically you can appreciate why we find it so hard to make heads or tails of your kind. We are generally referred to with just one term, whereas your sort always needs to be separated into gender). But let us return to the main point. A human being has a need to enrich his life, to seek companionship, security, whatever. This person has given some thought to the matter of sharing his home with one of us, has weighed advantages and disadvantages, studied several breeds, etc. etc. and then seemingly makes a choice.

WE: Seemingly?

MR. WOOF: Of course, because basically it is we who make the choice. If our new friend should, for example, not look acceptable or trustworthy, there are always ways to discourage a permanent relationship.

WE: Such as?

MR.WOOF: I really don't want to reveal all our secrets to you at this point. But surely you know yourself, one can bare one's teeth ferociously, growl, so that everyone thinks that we are rabid, or, this is the simplest way, we can pee against his leg.

WE: Well, so if you think that actually the choice of partner depends on you, then there should be nothing to object to at this point.

MR WOOF: That is a matter of attitude. Just think of how limited we are in the choice of our other future living companions. A young man meets a young woman, he hardly knows her, but she lets him kiss her under the apple tree, and voila, she moves in with him. Sometimes even for life, and there goes the peace and quiet of our original agreement. Or take the matter of children, which is often even worse. It appears that human beings are always in heat, and so children that then disturb the tranquility of the household are often the result of some sort of carelessness.

Has anyone ever considered that we have absolutely no vote in these matters?

WE: But in your case both nature and the person you have chosen to live with does have a vote?

MR.WOOF: Precisely. To be sure, I will admit that there are some of us who irresponsibly will chase after this or that hussy, but that is really because of the irresponsibility of our so-called master who does not watch over us with the same zeal with which we watch over him. Under proper, decent circumstances and conditions of bourgeois morality, the selection of and mating with an appropriate partner can be a very dignified procedure. After all, over the decades, even centuries, we have developed qualities and characteristics that can satisfy the highest demands.

WE: At the beginning of our conversation you stated that the operative word for your concerns is "Co-Determination." Just how do you envisage that this could be applied in these matters?

MR. WOOF: Well, in this sort of case it obviously all started with the kiss under the apple tree. We do not object if people wish to sniff each other out in this strange manner. However, if the relationship is to develop to greater intimacy from then on, we demand that we be involved in all further decisions.

WE: Just how would that proceed then?

MR. WOOF: A walk with the person in question through the streets, preferably a street of the individual's neighborhood. That would not only demonstrate the patience a person exhibits concerning our preference for stopping, sniffing, going on, stopping again, etc., but we might also be able to consult some of our colleagues in the neighborhood concerning the lifestyle of the applicant. As a matter of fact, we would even be willing to negotiate for a trial period of, let us say, four weeks. After all, we are modern and realize that in this day and age experimental relationships are not unheard of!

WE: And you are certain that under those circumstances you will be able to make a decision one way or another?

MR.WOOF: At least we will be able to determine whether our friend (whether male or female) has been barking up the wrong tree so to speak.

WE: If you don't mind, Mr. Woof, can we please return to a consideration of your initial relationship?

MR.WOOF: If you wish, of course.

WE: Suppose that while you are still available, so to say, because nobody has been worthy of you. What would your comment be if nobody had chosen you, rightly or wrongly, for whatever reason?

As you know, rejection can be practiced by both sides, and continued rejection can easily lead to severe psychological consequences.

MR.WOOF: Yes, you are quite right there. But one must also inquire into the reasons for such rejections. Is it not completely imaginable that one of us has not desired being tied to a home or to a single person? Surely you do not think that every unmarried woman has remained single because she has never found a man who wanted her. She simply chose to remain independent.

WE: That is true. But is there not a problem here? An unattached woman can get a job, even a good job these days, and that is how she will support herself for the rest of her life. However, your kind...

MR.WOOF: Doggone, you are doing it again. You seem to think that our only possible life is one where we depend on people. Just let me remind you of Lassie who supports an entire industry of people. Think of those of us who are devoted to serving mankind by sniffing explosives, drugs, finding people after avalanches, just to mention a few.

WE: Please forgive us. We have been thoughtless. Of course, you also support the police, serve the blind, amuse the elderly by bringing unconditional love and affection, you work in circuses....

MR.WOOF: You see. If we just doggedly pursue our campaign to point out to people what we are capable of, perhaps we can finally convince your kind that we are responsible enough to be granted official co-determination. Surely you must admit now, that we have been muzzled long enough.

WE: Yes, indeed! Can we now assume that we have touched upon the major reasons for the threatening restlessness in your circles?

MR.WOOF: Unfortunately not. While happily a good number of us live under reasonably satisfactory circumstances, given the present conditions, there are still too many who must lead an existence that is truly alien to their nature.

WE: Could you explain?

MR.WOOF: Surely. For example, think of those of us who sadly have wound up in the home of someone who cannot distinguish between our kind and a baby. I am thinking of those well-meaning ladies who insist on talking to us in baby talk and calling us with cutesy names, feeding us foods that are bad for us: candy, cookies, etc. 'Does little Putty want another big piece of this goody, goody cakypoo?' Pardon me; it's enough to make one throw up.

WE: Yes, I believe we all know the type. No need to dwell on it any further.

MR.WOOF: Gladly. But just let me point out that if we had the right of co-determination these situations could be avoided from the out-set. - But let me give you other examples. So many of these indignities take place at the dinner table. 'Here Cutesy-Poopsy, sit up and beg nicely.' Or this: The man of the house sits at a table and plays cards. Why must we sit right next to him? Why can't we stay in comfort on the sofa? In fact, there should be a law that those people who insist we sit right by their feet evening after evening must wash their feet more often. I don't mean to be indelicate, but I don't insist that they sniff us as is our custom.

WE: I see. There are cultural differences that we have simply ignored. You are right.

MR.WOOF: I'm afraid you have gotten me started. Think of this: The family likes to take a vacation somewhere on a beach in a tropical setting. Are we consulted when the trip is planned?

I happen to know a St. Bernard who originally lived in Labrador. This poor creature is forced to spend weeks every summer with his family in Mexico on a beach. And worse yet, they share their summer house with another family that brings along some ridiculous creature with-out any hair that yaps all day long.

WE: He would rather have remained at home in a kennel?

MR.WOOF: Why in a kennel? A small space with no room to move about, no comfort. Why not let him stay at home where he lives?

WE: All alone?

MR.WOOF: It would be preferable. But to be practical, people hire babysitters who come in and take care of the needs of a child, we are asking for no less.

WE: Once again, your demand seems reasonable.

MR.WOOF: You've now got me started. Think of the brutality when we have to wait in a closed car in the summer, while the lady of the house is in a comfortably air-conditioned supermarket.

WE: Is that really brutality or simply thoughtlessness?

MR. WOOF: Probably the former, but we perceive it as brutality just the same.

WE: And do people beat you?

WOOF: Unfortunately there are too many ignorant people who do. Still, there are, of course, ways for us to get back at them as long as we still have teeth.

WE: Isn't that a bit drastic?

MR.WOOF: To be sure, but at times necessary. And while we are at it, let us also talk about food.

WE: What about food?

MR.WOOF: Primarily we are the victims of an industry that pretends that it works in our interest and for our health.

WE: And they don't?

MR.WOOF: Sawdust! Dead horses that would do better to have become glue. Things you would never put into your stomachs. And we get it not only once in a while, but day after day as if we had no taste buds. All of this would change, if we had the right to come along into the store.

WE: The health laws! You can understand that, can't you?

MR.WOOF: Don't be ridiculous. Health laws, indeed! Have you ever heard of a man getting a cold from one of us? Rather the other way around I should think. No, the reason we are not allowed in a store is the result of a monopoly agreement by manufacturers of our foods. They have hired lobbyists who encourage pressure groups. If we could participate in a choice, they would soon go out of business.

WE: Forgive us, but we must ask you this: Are you a Communist?

MR. WOOF: Now that is pure nonsense. I know that it is said and written about us. Nothing but propaganda and lies. Just because we have a Russian greyhound on our board does not taint our entire organization. In fact, he is hardly a Communist, but indeed very rich from profits he has amassed racing in Florida.

WE: May we finally ask what your plans are for the future? Must we be fearful?

MR.WOOF: We must proceed in two ways. First of all, there are still too many of us who walk around with a hangdog expression. This sort of dog in the manger stance is contrary to our effort to make your kind aware of our natural born pride. We must therefore educate such unfortunate creatures and bring them into our fold.

WE: And then?

MR.WOOF: Of course, there are people who understand and are willing to stand with us. Unfortunately there are too many among them who are merely well-meaning do-gooders. People who think our lot will be much improved if they urge the civil authorities to install more fireplugs in our streets.

WE: Or trees?

MR.WOOF: Or trees. But, sad to say, we may actually have to think of force. I hate to sound as though I am threatening, and I live in the hope that perhaps this conversation has helped to create some sort of understanding and that we have come close to the end of our dog days.

WE: And you have hope?

MR.WOOF: Not necessarily.

WE: Would you really get aggressive? Bite or something like that?

MR.WOOF: Let me say that we prefer passive resistance. Suppose we would simply refuse for a time to go out on the street to do our business. Very soon people would be dog tired from forever cleaning up after us.

WE: True, but people might beat you.

MR.WOOF: Yes. Do you remember the famous philosopher who once said, 'The fool who fights has lost the argument'? I am afraid we must simply accept such action as a byproduct of our struggle. Surely you have heard of Gandhi?

WE: Naturally. Passive resistance.

MR.WOOF: Or barking at 2 o'clock at night, and again at 3 if necessary could achieve a whole lot. As an unexpected benefit it might even suppress the crime wave. Or tail wagging next to low coffee tables set for afternoon tea. Scratching in elevators and crowded places so that people think we have fleas. You have no idea how many ways there are to get on people's nerves.

WE: We have come to the end of our allotted time, Mr. Woof. Perhaps just one final word that can serve to sum up what we have discussed.

MR.WOOF: It's a dog's life!

WE: We thank you for this interview Mr. Woof.

LA BOULANGERIE

Now that Brigitte was on her way back, she had time to think about it all. Had it really been worth it, had it been as much fun as she had expected? She remembered how she had felt when she received the invitation to the ten-year reunion of her graduation from college. To see all of her former friends again, to learn what had happened to this one and that one; it had to be exciting. She had been a good student, not the top of her class, but not someone who had just made it either, so she had no reason to feel self-conscious now. For a couple of years after college she had kept up a correspondence with a few of her classmates, but then everybody seemed to have gotten too busy with their careers, with their lives, and so keeping in touch had simply fizzled out.

Not all of them of the class of '83 had been there, of course, even though there had only been 244 graduates that year; still there were enough of them to have made it worth the effort. But now, in retrospect, she wondered, 'Who were all these people?' Yes, she could recognize them physically, but in every other respect they were so different. A goodly number were quite fashionably dressed. Was that just for the occasion? Were they trying to prove something, to impress their former classmates? Quite a number of the girls were now either married (very successfully by all reports; the proof seemed to be baby pictures), or had a "live in"(to demonstrate their independence?) because no way would a husband and kids tie them down. Their careers came first, whatever that was. Yes, of course, there were some with higher degrees, some doctors, some lawyers, and a couple of them who were well on their way toward a professorship. She supposed one should have expected it from a few of them, although she could not remember that a couple had been particularly brilliant.

Perhaps the good of it was, that it forced one to take inventory of one's own life. Was she a success? Was she someone her classmates would brag about when they came home? Surely not. She was a secretary, a legal secretary to be sure, but even with the best of intentions one could not find anything particularly interesting about her career, if that is what one should call it. Hers was a conservative firm, and thus she was expected to dress conservatively, not to use too much make-up, to be soft spoken, unobtrusive, and quietly efficient. None of this she minded, it all suited her nature, and she had a right to feel that she was respected, considered reliable and efficient, and was even liked personally. All in all she was satisfied with her job.

Perhaps she should have bragged just a little more about the importance of her firm, of the cases which frequently were featured in the newspapers, but then, she hadn't gone there to brag, but to have a good time with old friends. Had her former roommate believed her when Brigitte assured her that she was happy, and, no she was not married, and no she had no particular boyfriend, because she wasn't really all that interested at this time? " I love my work and I love my independence." But the thought also crossed her mind "do I love my lonely Sundays, my vacations by myself". Maybe it would have been better if she had not gone.

The increasing traffic now demanded her full attention, and so it was not until much later in the evening that she continued to reflect on this day she had anticipated for so many weeks now. Perhaps she had gone about her remembrance of the events the wrong way. She had concentrated on the others. Perhaps the real value of such a get-together was that it should make you take stock of yourself. It had been obvious that what had most impressed her in the others ("there you go again, the others") had been the way they looked.

Brigitte began her inventory of herself in front of the bathroom mirror. Was she pretty? Does one even want to be 'pretty'? Somehow that has such a shallow sound, and fits little girls better than a woman in her early thirties. Good looking? Well, that is probably too much to ask for. Nice looking? Well, perhaps better 'not bad looking'. Maybe it would be an improvement if she changed her hairdo. There are those salons that can work miracles. And make-up! Yes, she had a lot to learn about make-up. She used a discreet lipstick, but she had never tried eyeshade or lashes. Department stores had those ladies in white or pink coats that put you in front of special mirrors and gave you a chance to try all sorts of tricks. And, oh yes, perfume. Very important. Just taking a bath every morning was obviously not enough.

What else? Of course, clothes. Naturally she would have to keep on dressing conservatively for her job, but there was such a thing as chic. Holly in the office knew about that, and one could surely ask her. Maybe her very high heels are just a bit too much, because ...ah yes, there is the matter of the figure. Nothing too much that can be done about that. Brigitte was just a bit on plump side. Not fat, but not a figure that makes men whistle. And her bosom? Men seemed to like that, and perhaps investing in some of those uplift bras might do something for her. And would she join one of those groups that exercises like mad after work? Probably not. She didn't want to become muscle-bound either. Then there is the question of where you can meet men without being blatantly floosy. Singles bars were out. Not that she had ever been to one, but the idea sounded like a meat market to her. Concerts? Libraries? Just sitting in the park? Quite a list and a lot to explore.

And explore she did. Within reason of course, nothing blatant, just a bit more lipstick today, more rouge tomorrow, a somewhat lower cut dress, heels a bit higher, a try at a fragrance. Then tickets to the theatre, concerts, even opera, but none of this resulted in any more than the momentary polite pleasantry with people who remained strangers, and even the occasional male who was clearly looking for no more than an immediate one night stand.

What is it with men? Didn't anyone out there look for no more than pleasant company, conversation, exchange of opinions and ideas? How did people find each other? There was only one man she could ask about men, her brother. It wasn't all that easy to see him because he was a baker and his hours were so different from her own. He was already long at work when she got up, and when she was done with her work he was about to get out of bed to go to work. Still, he was married, and Brigitte knew that he was happy.

Of course Otto was surprised to see his sister at 6 o'clock in the morning in his shop.

"Is there something wrong?"

"No," Brigitte assured him, "not really. It's just that we don't see each other much at any other time, and I couldn't sleep, and so I thought I'd stop in."

"Great." He smiled at her. He really liked his sister. "How about giving me a hand here while we talk?" he suggested.

A bakery early in the morning is a great place. Everything smells so sweet, so inviting. There is nothing like the fragrance of freshly baked bread. The next couple of hours passed easily, so that she almost was surprised when she looked at her watch.

"Heavens, Otto. I've got to go to work. It's already late, and thanks for the talk."

"That's O.K., Come back when you can," he said, "sorry that I couldn't help your friends with an idea."

The friends had, of course, been an invention so that she could ask what was on her mind without embarrassment. As it had turned out, he hadn't helped her. He had never much thought about man as a subject matter. And he had married Lisa because he was in love with her, and that was it. How had it happened? "It just did," he had said. "It just felt right".

It was too late to go home again, and somewhat breathless she caught the elevator up to the office just in time. One of the young lawyers of her firm had squeezed in next to her, and when he recognized her, he smiled. Later that morning, quite unexpectedly, he stopped at her desk and asked whether she might join him for a drink after work. He seemed nice about it and so she accepted, even though she was a bit puzzled that he had suddenly noticed her. They had spoken before on business many times. Maybe she'll ask him while they are having this drink.

Of course, she didn't. It had been a nice evening, and they even went to dinner together, but when the next morning she told him "It was so nice, I had a really good time," he just said "I'm so glad" rather than "So did I, let's do it again." Something had gone wrong. She had failed, and so life went on in its own drab way.

It was the Saturday before Labor Day when Otto called very early in the morning. His helper had decided to make a long weekend of it, could she perhaps come and help. She had done it before, and while she had planned to sleep late, how could she turn down her brother in trouble. Besides, it wasn't really hard work, and she had always enjoyed the wonderful odors of the bake shop. In fact, she even stayed an extra couple of hours to help out in the store.

On her way home she stopped at the supermarket. On a holiday restaurants were so crowded that one felt conspicuous as a single person looking for a table. Somehow hostesses had a way of saying: "Just one?" in a somewhat accusatory tone. Brigitte was going to cook for herself. Just as she was staring into the meat counter she heard a voice behind her: "Hi!" It was Tony, Tony her classmate with whom she had exchanged no more than five words at the reunion.

"Well, hello. This is a surprise Tony. Shopping for the family?"

"Just for myself, Brigitte. I live alone. Do you come here often?"

"Only when I get the urge to cook, and this is the kind of weekend when I feel that urge," she said.

"I know what you mean. Restaurants prefer families, groups on days like that, and they look at you kind of funny when you ask for a table for one."

How nice. There is someone who thinks just like I do. I really don't know anything about him after we graduated. And so as they pushed their carts along the isles, conversation developed easily. He actually liked to cook, at least so it seemed. Of course he was a chemist, and from what she remembered of Chem 1, they like to combine all sorts of ingredients to have it come out as something else.

Tony laughed when she expounded on her analysis of chemistry in relationship to cooking. "Still, there's a lot of truth in it," he encouraged her. "I work for a firm that makes perfumes, fragrances of all sorts, and when I cook I want it to be a pleasure for my nose as well as my taste buds."

"I'd be scared to death to cook for you," Brigitte observed.

And then she was surprised when he said, "Then don't. Let's just have a picnic if you have the time and would like to."

"My gosh, that would be great and I'd like it very much. I can get some cold cuts and stuff, and I already have some fresh rolls from my brother's bakery."

"Believe it or not, I can smell that. So, I'll bring some fruit and some wine, and if you give me your address, I'll pick you up in a couple of hours."

It was such a wonderful weekend, and they spent every waking moment of it together. He was kind, considerate; he did not rush her, and when asked whether she would spend a weekend in the mountains with him, she realized that she had known for some time already that she would say "yes". And she did not regret it for a moment, but when she lay happy and secure in his arms, she thought of the ten years they had wasted without each other. How did it happen now, why had it not happened then. Can one, should one ask at a moment like this why he had suddenly been attracted to her after all of this time?

When she asked the question, he laughed. "You'll never believe this," he explained, "but you know now where I work and what I do. All day long I keep smelling perfumes, in beakers, in bottles, on models who try them out. Some of these smells are quite exotic, some much too loud and penetrating, some rather delicate and gentle and lovely fragrances, but basically they are all artificial. And there you were in that supermarket, and even before you told me so, I could smell that odor of freshly baked bread, that lovely healthy fragrance."

"And that is why you love me? I smell good and you'll keep loving me as long as I carry fresh rolls around with me?"

"Of course not, Darling," he chuckled, "although that may not be a bad idea. But seriously, it was what attracted me, and I'm damn glad it did, because it gave me the chance to get to know the person behind that fragrance."

They appeared together at the next reunion. Fifteen years this time, and nobody ignored her this time. They all knew who Brigitte was; it was a name known all over the world now. She and Tony had opened the world to all those girls who had not been born glamour girls, who did not have the perfect figure, but who were so very nice, so very lovable, if only someone would take the trouble to discover them. Their perfume with her name on it made use of what had been known ever since men and women inhabited the world: a man's love does not reside in his heart, but in his stomach, all one had to do is to find the secret that connects the one to the other. Their fragrance of freshly baked bread had swept the world markets in an unbelievably short time. Indeed it was not unusual to hear psychologists and sociologists pontificate on TV Talk Shows that LA Boulangerie (perfumes have to have French names in order to succeed) was well on its way to change the moral climate of the world as a result of its healthy impact, and were well on the way to saving the American family.

STRANGERS

It was a lovely late afternoon and the deep blue sky, with its few wisps of clouds, held the promise of a perfect weekend. The highway was choked with cars leaving the city, but somehow it seemed to Will as though traffic was flowing more easily than usual. The annoyance he so often felt about having to share the road with so many unpredictable others, had today given way to the feeling that he was engaged in a friendly competition with those in the other three lanes , all of them with the same happy sense that soon they would be home, with their families, relaxed, enjoying the fruits of their labors of the past week.

For several traffic lights now he had stopped next to the same cars. The drivers had glanced quickly at each other on the first stop. As the intervals between lights grew longer, their looks at finding each other again side-by-side a mile later turned into smiles. Will picked up the tune from another man's car and whistled to the music as he tapped his foot on the floorboard. A few times his line moved faster than that of the others and with a triumphant smile he rolled ahead of his competitors before he came to a stop. He was proud that he shared his line with the better drivers. But then, soon "his line" fell behind again, and he cursed those slowpokes in front of him, felt let down, and quite alone again. With a flourish he negotiated the last curve to the exit and then turned off unto the country lane, which led to his house as he honked his horn three times as a parting gesture.

On the lane it was peaceful. Here the countryside could show off its beauty without interference from billboards and gas stations. At this moment, nothing in this world could have warned him of the impending disaster he would face.

As he turned into the driveway he saw his two children, Marjorie, 11, and Jimmy, 13, playing in front of the house. He was proud of them, and through them of himself as they came running to greet him. With one of them at each side, he walked into his house, and stopped in surprise. There was his wife, the impeccable housekeeper Val in the middle of the living room floor with a mountain of papers pulled out of his desk drawers surrounding her. Her usual affectionate greeting was today simply a curt, "Hello, dear."

"Val, what in the world has happened?" Will asked. She never even looked up at him: "I'm trying to find something." Will was relieved. For a moment he had thought of burglars. He carefully picked his way through the debris and began to laugh: "This is like in the fairy tale when the prince must fight his way through the hedge to kiss his beloved." He towered over her and pulled her up close to him. "You can stop looking, Snow White, you've found your prince charming." He kissed her, but the response he got was only dutiful and mechanical without the same joy he had put into it.

"I'm sorry," Val said. "I'll straighten this up and get supper. She then plunged back into her preoccupied hustle as though he had never entered the room.

"Can I help you?"

"No, thanks."

"What are you looking for, dear? Perhaps I know where it is," Will suggested.

But his wife was uncommunicative. "Nothing, I'll find it." He didn't bother to joke that nothing could probably not be found anywhere since he doubted that she would find it amusing. Feeling unwanted, he retreated to the porch and barricaded himself behind his newspaper following the age-old custom of puzzled husbands.

Supper was a drab affair, having that wholesale taste of all canned foods and lacking the careful culinary composition which had put considerable poundage on Will since his marriage. The conversation at the table seemed to take its cue from the uninspired fare and featured long periods of blandness. Will thought it best to drop the matter of the lost object for the time being and tried to entertain his family with the events of the day. But it takes an enthusiastic audience to make a good teller of tales. Even the children seemed to be affected by the imponderable mood of the house and were remarkably good and quiet. He almost wished they would do some kind of fool thing so he could shout at them.

Val hardly said three words. She gulped down her food and waited rather impatiently for the rest of them to finish. As soon as the last plate was emptied, she excused herself and got up without keeping Will company for his after-dinner cigarette and second cup of coffee. She knew that he loved this part of the meal particularly because he felt warm and comfortable since the children generally excused themselves to go outside or upstairs. As often as not this was the time when plans were discussed about the family, vacations, the house, or a new car, and better yet, dreams of fancy were spun into the web of the future. Often they sat like this for an hour or more since the children were old enough to go to bed by themselves. None of that happened tonight. Val disappeared upstairs into the bedroom without a word and left her husband to his own devices.

'It'll blow over,' he thought. 'She'll find whatever it is soon and then probably feel very silly about it.' It was hard to spoil his good mood tonight, and so he went out to play catch with the children in the backyard. However, they were through playing catch and showed no inclination to go back to it. Whatever their new game was, there seemed to be no use for their father in it. He moodily settled down on the front steps, aching for some neighbor to come along so that he could talk to him, but the street remained deserted. Just as he was about to go in the children joined him, now tired of their game and ready for a story. Will was no storyteller however, and so he tried conversation. He always found it much harder to talk to the children than to any grown-up. They were nice kids, to be sure, and they were after all his family, but he could not shed that feeling of self-consciousness when he was alone with them. Things were all right when they asked questions, but tonight there were none and they seemed to expect him to take the lead. And so mechanically he asked about school, about their teachers, their friends, what they had learned this week, but he had the distinct feeling that there was little interest in those topics. Suddenly it occurred to him that they might know what mysterious object was about to spoil his entire weekend. They didn't. All they could report was that their mother had been to a tea party at Stella Herman's house, and that when she came home had immediately started on her search.

He went upstairs to his bedroom but this time found his wife buried under the contents of several dresser drawers. He sat down on his bed. "Val," he began, "Val, please tell me what this is all about. Isn't it just possible that I know where the damned thing is?"

"Don't swear, Will," she said.

"All right, but isn't it possible?"

"No."

He started another line of questioning. "Well, even if I don't, does it have to be a secret what it is?"

"It's no secret."

"It is to me."

"I wish you wouldn't smoke in the bedroom, Will," Val admonished him. He looked for a place to squash his cigarette but there wasn't any. Furiously he stomped out of the room leaving his footprints on two clean sheets and a towel on the floor. For the next few hours he heard her rummaging through the house. In the attic he heard her moving some trunks, and in the basement she later dropped a heavy drawer of one of the file cabinets they kept there. He considered helping her, but a stubborn streak kept him in his chair. The children had long since gone to bed. He read the entire paper once more without really reading it, and even studied the want ads, marveling at what people buy and sell and the prices they ask and seem to get nowadays. For a while he tried television, but the sit-corns were not funny tonight, and the films seemed to be from an era when makeup looked like faces dipped into a barrel of flour plus a very black smear to indicate lips .He felt this made any show of emotion impossible because a smile or grief would have without question cracked the floury paste on the cheeks, and so actresses of that day were limited to a flutter of elongated eyelashes as a standard reaction to any situation. The men were equally standardized with their too dark eye shading and patent leather hair, which through the ages carried the faint suggestion of rancid goose fat, hero and villains were distinguished by means of a mustache,.

Will turned the set off. It was 10:30 and he was going to go to bed. He announced his plans down into the basement, adding an invitation to join him. It was declined.

On the way up he noticed that the supper dishes were still on the table and the odor of the left-over bits and pieces settled insidiously over the whole downstairs.

Val came up three hours later and went straight to be without the customary nocturnal ablutions, which had always puzzled him so much but also flattered him because he assumed they were for his benefit. Not a word was spoken though he longed to slide over to her side and put his arms around her. Somehow he knew he would be rebuffed. With a tremendous bounce he threw himself on his stomach and arranged himself for the rest of the night. Morning came and brilliant sunshine flooded the room. Saturday morning is so much nicer than Sunday, because there is the knowledge that this is only the beginning, for a whole day, to be followed by another when one can be the master of his own time. Will was not a lazy man and when he worked he worked hard and with apparent success. But when he rested he wanted to be correspondingly lazy without any interference.

Val was already up and out of the room. Her absence reminded him forcefully of the events of yesterday. He sat up and looked at his clock. 8:30 already. Of course, she is up and probably already found "it" and everything is forgotten, and all he had to do was to go down and kiss her and not mention a word about it and the weekend would be fine. She was in the kitchen doing the dishes. Last night's leftover dishes, and unheard of thing in her household.

"Beautiful morning, darling" he announced cheerfully and brushed his cheek against hers.

"Good morning, Will. You scratch."

"Of course I scratch; I'm the original caveman; didn't you know? I've come to drag you to breakfast by your beautiful curls, my sweet.

"It's all set in there for you, and the coffee is on the warm plate," she informed him.

"Aren't you coming.?"

"I've had mine with the children. They've gone on a picnic for the day with the Bergsons."

"Say, that's a swell idea. Why don't you have another cup of coffee, and then I'll help you with the dishes and we'll go out to lunch some nice place?" He beamed all over with anticipation.

"I'm sorry, Will. I still have a few things to do around the house, and besides I'll have to go to town."

He did not try to hide his disappointment. "What for?"

"To look for something at my mother's house," Val said. And that was the end of that.

He spent the morning puttering around the garden and watched a ballgame in the afternoon. When Val came back toward evening, he noticed that she had been crying. Without so much as a greeting, she went into the kitchen and was obviously very busy.

The quality of the supper was not much better this evening, but the children were full of experiences and so it did not seem quite so much like a death watch. He and Val ignored each other studiously and soon after supper he took his car and went out for a long ride.

When he got home he marched straight up to his bedroom. Val was some-where about, but he wasn't interested. He immediately went to bed and fell asleep without even turning over. He woke up at 3 a.m. with a slightly uneasy feeling. Val was not there. Her bed had not been slept in but he pillow and blankets were gone. He found her on the sofa in the living room, awake and bathed in tears.

"What's the matter, honey?" he asked tenderly.

All he got for an answer was sobbing.

"Can't you tell me? Isn't there any way in which I can help you?"

She just moaned.

"Come on, darling, it can't be anything so terrible that I shouldn't know about it. After all, I am your husband."

A heavy sigh preceded a new fit of crying. He really felt sorry for her, but damn it all, how could he help her if she just bawled and didn't say anything.

"Come on to bed now. We'll talk about it in the morning," he said trying to be somewhat firmer in his voice.

But when he reached for her to help her up she turned away and shouted, "Leave me alone!"

Will forgot about being sympathetic and went upstairs where he spent the rest of the night without any sleep.

When he got up he shaved and dressed quite carefully before he went down to breakfast. He was determined that today he was going to settle this mysterious business once and for all. She was already there, but he held back until the children were off to Sunday school.

"All right, now," he said quite sternly to Val, "let's go into the living room"

Much to his surprise she followed without an argument. They sat opposite from each other, the coffee table between them.

"All right now, Val. This business has been going on for two days now, and I don't mind telling you that I am getting pretty tired of it all. If there is something wrong I ought to know about it. We have never had any se-crets from each other, and we are sensible people, and I don't think that there is anything so terrible that you could have done that I don't know about it.

Val looked smaller in her chair than she actually was. Her eyes were red and she kept touching her nose with her handkerchief.

"All right, Will," she sobbed, "I would have had to tell you today anyway. It's...it's...oh, I can't...it's too terrible."

She cried again.

Will got up and sat down next to her and reached for her hand. He tried to be very gentle and fatherly.

"Don't touch me, please, don't touch me," Val whimpered.

He retreated. "Let's try it this way," he began once more. "Now on Friday morning when I left you were all right. Then in the afternoon you went to a party at Stella's house. Did you get there all right without trouble?"

She nodded.

So it wasn't an accident at least, Will thought. "Now, who all was there?"

Laboriously she counted: "Stella, and Mary Haron, and Mrs. Petucci and her daughter, and... oh, Sybil Schmitz and Stella's cousin Rita and her new husband Frank."

"O.K., now what did you talk about?"

"Oh, this and that. Mostly women's talk."

"That must have been charming for Rita's new husband." Then he tried to put her at ease and asked, "What kind of a guy is he, anyway?"

"All right."

"Young? Old?"

"Very young."

"What's his business?" Not that he cared at the moment, but perhaps talking about someone else would distract her.

"They just got back from their honeymoon," Val informed him.

Even though she didn't answer his question, he was willing to play it her way. "Where did they go? And did they have a good time?"

She hesitated with the answer, "Well...I guess....no, they didn't."

"Oh, what's the matter?"

Much to his surprise Val suddenly straightened up and looked right square at him. "They were driving," she said, "and the first night they stopped at a Motel. After they registered the man behind the desk looked at their name and then asked if they could prove that they were married." Val slumped back to her former position of despair.

"Could they?" he encouraged her.

"No."

"And so?"

Suddenly she looked outraged. "And so, you say! And so the man didn't rent them a room and since it was late they had to take two rooms at opposite ends."

Will chuckled. This turned out to be quite different than what he might have expected. "And so Frank got caught visiting his own wife on his wedding night, and they threw him into the town jail in his nighty for indecent conduct," he suggested.

"He didn't get caught." Val was not amused. "He didn't go to her at all."

"That's serious," Will admitted. "So now they are unhappy about it, and feel this is a serious omen?"

She shook her head. "No, they think it's funny."

"And you don't?"

"No, I don't."

"How come they couldn't prove they were married anyway?"

"They had forgotten their license before they left."

Ah, he began to understand that part of it all right. These kids probably looked pretty young still, and the man at the motel was a little too careful for once. But what in the world did all of this have to do with her problem? He asked her.

She began to cry again. Softly. The she explained how on the way home she had thought about this story, and how she had begun to wonder where their marriage certificate was. And then suddenly she had become aware of how terrible it would be if it were lost. Ever since then she had been looking all over the house, and then she had even gone to her mother's place just in case. But now she was sure that the paper was lost for good. Will was thunderstruck. So that was it? Because of an eight-year-old piece of paper the peace of the entire household had been disturbed. Then he started to laugh, loud and long until there were tears in his eyes.

Val stared at him in disbelief. "Do you think it's funny not being married to me?"

"Who the hell says I'm not?"

"You can't prove it."

"Who wants me to? Aren't you sure?" He was still drying the tears from his eyes.

"That's not at all the point. Nobody wants you to prove it today perhaps, but we don't know about tomorrow. What if we had been at that motel and the man would have asked you?"

"Oh, sure, you and I and the kids. Anyway, I would have knocked his block off."

"Be serious Will, I mean it," Val threatened.

He composed himself. "All right, dear, perhaps I wouldn't have right then and there, but nobody is going to ask an old buck like me in the first place. These kids perhaps, but not us."

"I'd be embarrassed to death."

"I don't know. I think it would be quite romantic. After all, Val, that would put you right into the vamp class." He wished he could make her see the humor of it all. "Besides, people don't generally go around and carry their wedding license with them."

"Oh, Will, please. There are a thousand chances someone may want to see it. Now just imagine the children in school are asked to bring their parent's marriage license for show and tell. Just imagine what would Marge and Jimmy do? They'd be shunned by all the other children, and the teachers would look pityingly at them, and soon the people in the neighborhood would begin to whisper that we are living in sin."

Will didn't quite see why the school would want such a thing anyway. "But even if," he continued, "even if I simply go to the principal and tell him that we have lost our license, and

if he wants to see your driver's license or whatever else you have with our name on it, we'll send him that. Now, I am sure we are not the first couple that has mislaid an important paper."

"You can give any name you want to on a driver's license. They never check up. It would be no good."

"All right then, how about a duplicate? Can't you go to the Reverend Schoener and get a duplicate?"

"It wouldn't be the same," she said.

"Why not? Is there something especially holy about the original?"

"Of course there is, it's the most important piece of paper in my life." She started to sob again. "Besides, our witness Jim Brown got killed and so nobody could sign for him."

At that point the children came back from church. Val quickly tried to wipe away her tears and dashed out into the kitchen. Will listened absentmindedly to a narration about Noah and the animals on which Jimmy had reported.

"Is that so," he said ever so often when it seemed time for a comment, and it was enough to keep his son going.

He just couldn't understand why all of this was such a problem. After all, it was only a piece of paper. Maybe an important one even, but there were plenty of people still alive that had witnessed their wedding. Nobody had ever questioned it in eight years, and now they had two children, a home, and suddenly someone should suspect that it was all illegal? Ridiculous.

And besides, in this day and age there were plenty of people with children who hadn't gotten married. One read about such things in the tabloid headlines at the supermarket, and nobody really gave a damn.

A drink restored his first point of view. It was all just ridiculous. Maybe this is what she needed; maybe a drink would make her see it in the right perspective. He walked into the kitchen glass in hand, but Val declined.

When Sunday dinner was on the table only the clatter of knives and forks could be heard, until Will suddenly startled them all with roaring laughter. He coughed and choked and became quite red in the face and then pointed at his children. "You poor little bastards" he shouted," you poor..."

Jim and Marge stared at him wide-eyed and Val turned as white as a sheet. Without a word of warning, she got up and left the room. Will stormed after her.

"Now look here, Val."

"You're drunk."

"Nonsense, I don't get drunk from one little drink...don't you see, Val?" he pleaded.

"Of course, I see...of course. They are bastards. That's what people will say. You've said it already." The rest of her sentence was lost in tears.

He was stone sober. "Now listen. I've had enough of all of this nonsense. None of these things are going to happen in the first place so it's no problem anyway. Besides, if you remember, we got married because we loved each other and not so that we could have a piece of paper with our name on it. We still love each other and up until Friday we were happy and a piece of paper had nothing to do with it."

"It's free love! It's immoral."

"Rot. You and I know we were married and that is all that matters, and we'll continue to love each other and be happy, paper or no paper."

"That's not enough."

"Why not?"

"We can't prove it to the children."

"We don't have to."

"We may have to. Some day. They may ask."

"If they do, I'll pin their ears back. And even if they do, we'll explain it to them, and maybe some day when they inherit the house they find our license somewhere in the basement or the attic. Besides, even if we were not married, they love us because they are a piece of us. Nothing can change that."

"Children are a responsibility," she sniffled gravely, "they can't be brought up properly by pinning their ears back. They can demand answers from us and it is our responsibility to have our house in order for them."

He was quite unable to follow her. Somehow it all seemed unreal as though they were saying someone else's lines on a stage. Val had always been a little prim and proper, had known that even before they were married. But this he had never expected.

"What do you suggest we do?" he inquired.

"There is only one thing we can do."

"And that is?"

"The children and I will have to leave."

"Val!" he got up, "you can't be serious."

"Of course I am." She was very composed now.

"And just where would you go? To your mother's?"

Val shook her head in agony. "No, not there. People would know and then it would all come out much sooner."

"Where then?"

"I don't know. West, to some other state where no one knows me and I can get a job and people will think I'm a widow."

"But you are not. And what if someone asks you?"

"I'd tell them just that."

"Isn't that lying too?"

"Of course it is, but it would have to be for the sake of the children." She had all the answers.

"And what about me?" he asked. "What am I to do?"

"Naturally, you'll divorce me. Quietly, I hope."

He didn't dare point out to her that if they weren't married he could not possibly divorce her. It would make no impression.

"I'll roast in hell first," he said grimly.

"Then I'll have to do it, and I'll tell people I am divorced and bear the shame as punishment for my sins."

"Another idea occurred to him. He would divorce her all right if that was what she wanted, and the next day they would get married again. In the meantime he would court her just as he had nine years ago. In the meantime she would sort of be his mistress.

"No," she said.

"Why not? You married me once."

"I wouldn't again. Not after this."

"Good god, Val, I haven't changed any since yesterday, have I?"

"Perhaps you haven't, but maybe I never really knew you."

"And now you do?"

"Yes, now I do."

"And how am I?"

"Flippant, irresponsible and immoral," she said firmly.

"All right," he gave in to her. "I'm sorry I thought it was funny when you didn't. I should have had sense enough to humor you, but I do love you, Val."

"There are worlds between us that can't be bridged any more."

"All that is between us is a missing piece of paper," he reminded her.

"That piece of paper, as you call it, is the world to me."

"No, it isn't," Will insisted. "It represents one, but the home and the children and our love that is the world. If we didn't have all that and only a piece of paper you would be right."

"So you see," she said

That threw him completely off his track. He just shrugged his shoulders in despair. "O.K. if that is what you want. But you stay here and I'll go and get a room in town. In a few days I'll come back and we can talk about it then."

"You won't find me here," Val said.

"Why not? Aren't you comfortable here?"

"I couldn't stay alone with you in the same house. It would be wrong."

Naturally it would. They were suddenly strangers now and the past years of sharing the same bedroom are not as important as the damned bureaucratic certificate whose absence even forbade them to share the same house chaperoned. Suddenly it all annoyed him beyond measure.

Without further comment, he went, packed a bag, and left the house.

He was sitting on the edge of the bathtub concentrating on the foam that was building up in the tub. Just another moment and he would submerge himself into this soft, white bed of cotton. Slowly, as always, because the water was very hot, just as he loved it. He would stretch out very gingerly until only his head and his knees were still visible. As long as he could remember the hot tub had been his favorite place for dreaming. Already as a child he had discovered that in this room you could lock yourself away from the world, that here nobody would disturb you, interrupt you. After all cleanliness was a generally applauded attribute. He made use of this although being clean was not his primary motivation. That could be achieved much more quickly under a shower. No, what he was after was a quiet, secluded, undisturbed place for thinking. That is what he called it if he talked about it at all because it sounded more important, more serious that dreaming, because he knew well that he rarely followed a thought to its conclusion. Generally he began with a question that had occurred to him sometime during the day, but soon enough all logic, all organized thought seemed to dissolve in this primordial ooze; he drifted, his mind only occasionally formed real words, even the occasional brief sentence, nothing coherent, nothing organized, nothing real.

Some time ago he had described this feeling to a friend of his. A student of psychology who immediately concluded that he was afraid of life; that at the bottom of all of this he yearned to return to the warmth of his mother, before he was born, when he swam safely protected in the amnion fluid of her body. He had rejected this interpretation as revolting and completely off the mark. For one thing it revolted him to think of his mother in this way, and on the other hand he considered himself to be someone who quite consciously and happily occupied his place in life. He was 23 years old and he liked it. But to be young again, very young, that he desired in no way.

Well, the time came, he would now turn off the water and begin the ritual. As always his thoughts turned to Japan at these moments. He heard that there people took these very hot baths, and he had often wondered whether he would ever be able to travel to this far away land to see whether he could stand this too. But then, as far as he knew people there bathed in public and that was a real problem. Oh, not because he was ashamed to be seen naked, but the real attraction of this whole exercise lay in the fact that you could lock the door to shut out the world outside. Now there was a problem that he absolutely had to think about today, think about, not dream.

He knew what it was like, Helga had once visited him in the tub: Helga whom he would marry tomorrow. They had spent the evening in a discotheque with friends, had danced and it had grown late. Somehow, after all it was Saturday and he would not have to get up early tomorrow morning, somehow he had decided not to drive her that long way home but took her along to his apartment. No, let's be honest, it was not by chance, he had planned it and besides it was not the first time that she had stayed with him over night even though her parents seemed not to be too happy about it. They did not say so, but one could notice it.

No doubt they said to themselves, without really convincing themselves, "Well, times are different today and people think different about moral things than in our day. And besides, perhaps those young people are right and in that way avoid disappointments later on. Anyway, it looks as though they are thinking about marrying." And then without saying so in words they thought 'I just hope nothing happens' which meant of course that Helga would not get pregnant.

Well now, on that evening they were just about to take their clothes off when Helga suddenly suggested "Why don't we take a bath together? You could wash my back if you want to," and as she said it there was a bit of an invitingly suggestive smile on her lips. Actually the suggestion made a good bit of sense because it had been quite hot at the dance and they both had perspired a good bit. But the idea that someone would break into his secret life had never occurred to him until just that moment. He tried excuses that after all they had the entire weekend ahead of them and should take time to proceed to lovemaking slowly, and besides he was really quite exhausted and tired. Wouldn't it be better to wait perhaps until tomorrow morning. How about taking a quick shower for now? But none of that had made any impression on her, and soon she had convinced him that a nice hot bath would surely stimulate him, especially if they would be in the tub together. How can you say no to a girl you love, and it was real that he loved her although he was not quite certain that he actually knew what love was. And indeed, he soon also realized to his surprise that Helga had been right. It was stimulating even though he first had had to overcome some reticence. In fact, he had not quite realized it at the time that the time of experimentation was over, and very soon now they should set the date for a permanent alliance.

But now all of that looked quite different again. Was it possible today was the last time that he could enjoy the luxury of his solitary bath with all that was part of it? Even though one could assume that starting tomorrow Helga would not want to share the tub with him every time, from tomorrow on into all eternity. Would she understand it when he disappeared into just this room, lock the door and not reappear for one and a half hours? Would she get used to the thought this was simply one his little peculiarities, the sort that one could not have predicted before marriage? Harmless, actually, at least until there are children. It's probably all right as long as they are babies. But when they get to be 14 or 15 , especially if they are girls who are notoriously glued to bathroom mirrors, then what? A horrible thought.

He let the white foam run through his fingers. Ever so slowly, almost like a sticky mass it dripped through his finger and formed a mountain on a clear spot on the surface of the water. It was as though for just a moment a hole had opened and through this hole he could see his own body. He shook his hand so that the foam would fall away from it just a little faster, so that he could cover his nakedness more quickly. The thought had just come to him that it was perhaps this body that was to be blamed for this dilemma. Was this love he felt for Helga or perhaps nothing other than an intoxication of the moment, yearning merely for satisfaction for his own body? Was he simply the victim of his own dreams and musings?

He now remembered, two years ago when he had hardly gotten to know her, it was soon after that that he had first kissed her, their third date as he remembered it but their first kiss. Yes, after that he had also sunk into his bath and abandoned himself to his thoughts, thoughts about her, about this girl who had not only accepted his kiss as others had after a nice evening together, but who had returned it firmly and at the same time softly as if she meant to say "yes, this is good, your mouth and mine belong together". And from that feeling came a dream, which she gave herself to him, quite simply, quite naturally without any hesitation although it was obviously the first time for her. And when later this dream turned into reality it quite surprised him since after all generally his dreams did not turn into reality.

Perhaps that's what it was. Perhaps he had looked upon the first time as well as all the other times when they had been together "like that" simply as the continuation of his dreams.

But, of course, Helga had now destroyed these dreams when she has urged him to let her join him in his bath. Was he perhaps a man who could not live in the real world? no, that could not be, that must not be. After all, up to now he had always managed to stand up to everyday life. He had studied, Sociology, not all the way to a degree, but far enough to be able to converse intelligently about its general problems. And during the semester break he had worked with his hands and managed there too to get along with people in those circles. For the last eight months he had a job in a bank and was generally regarded as reliable and it was expected that he would get ahead quite rapidly. His father had died when he was only twelve years old and since the small pension from the railroad was hardly enough for his mother to live on, she had had to go to work to take care of herself and her son. She had earned his way through high school as a waitress, and since she often had to work in the evening, he had gotten used to cooking for himself and often also helped her on her day off with work around the house. In other words, he had very much grown up in the real world. This dreaming in which he indulged himself even then was nothing but a kind of luxury, a sort of game with his imagination just as other people go to the movies for the same reason. They had not been able to afford a television set at that time, so it was up to him to invent something to indulge his imagination.

Now Helga, she had grown up in quite a different way. Her father owned a factory. Shoes. He had built it up all on his own after the war because he was a man of enormous energy and willpower. In short, he was someone one had to admire. He had come from a family of simple working people but he did not seem to be ashamed of that, and he had not even graduated from High School and did not have to hide that either. I seems he had read a great deal and in any case he had a real instinct for business. Had he always been like that? People who knew even when they were very young lust where they wanted to go are really to be envied. On the other hand he probably had not known it or he would have married a different woman. Not that there was anything especially wrong about Helga's mother, quite the contrary, she was a very lovable and simple person- the very model of a housewife whose world is made up of nothing other than worry about her family. In other words she was a good woman, but not a lady of the sort that would have been more appropriate to a successful businessman. At receptions and parties she was clearly uncomfortable and unhappy, yet it has to be noted that Mr. Binger was by no means ashamed of her. He did not need that. If a man such as he chooses a wife such as she is, it had to be the right thing to do.

It was in this well-to-do even rich world that Helga had grown up, and since she remained the only child (did that perhaps indicate a lack of success for Mr. Binger?) she was the apple of her parent's eyes. Never did her father deny her smallest wish, not even those she had not yet expressed and for that reason he had probably not even opposed her choice of partner in marriage, though he could hardly have been the choice of their dreams. Her mother was more of a servant than a parent to her, was ready with a hot meal regardless of when she came home, did her laundry, though the family of course had servants, drove her to school every morning even after her daughter had learned to drive, even though she herself was afraid of driving.

With all of this, it would hardly have been surprising if Helga found it hard to cope with reality since after all she had never really experienced it. She should have become the dreamer, not her. Could it be that she was one? Even though they had been so very close for some time now, she did not know about his secret life; possibly he knew nothing about hers.

The suspicion arose in his mind that it was precisely because she herself also knew about the danger of musing in the tub from her own experience and that was why she had enticed him that day to join him. What could that mean?

Perhaps she wanted to say "From now on we will dream together" or perhaps the opposite "from today on bathing is something that has to do with the body, only the body, with yours and with mine. Dreaming entails too many dangers that one might also dream about something else, someone else, about another life.

Suddenly he became aware that the water had grown quite cool. He was used to that, it was hardly surprising, and all that was required was to turn on the hot water tap to raise the temperature again. It was an almost automatic gesture and he always left room for it when he first filled the tub. But this time he had not noticed that he was actually sitting up straight until this moment. When he leaned back again he bent his knee so that it was still showing above the sea of foam that had formed again.

An island, surrounded by a white, snowy mass of icebergs, only that these icebergs did not cause you to freeze. Many years ago, before he had not yet tried a bubble bath, he had often used a nailbrush to float lazily toward this island. He was still young and the island had become a tropical pirate's hiding place in a huge ocean. Once he had mastered the trick of moving the water with a slight motion of his toes, one could create surf and even a storm, whatever seemed appropriate at the moment. This nailbrush had survived many dangerous journeys.

Naturally now he was too old for this sort of game, but the island remained and fulfilled other purposes. One could flee from everyday lie, begin a new life which naturally encompassed an idyllic existence. It was a sort of Slaraffia the land of milk and honey the inhabitants of which were mostly pretty young girls who cheerfully and in entirely uncomplicated ways would fulfill your every desire.

To lose yourself on such a fantasy island, to flee from every responsibility, yes also from the one which he was to assume tomorrow for the rest of his life. Certainly she would cry for a few days, and then everything would go over into great anger because he had left her standing at the altar so to speak. But she would calm down again and soon he would be forgotten. In fact her mother would probably be happy to be able to care for her daughter for a while longer, and the father, this admirable man, would in this situation too through his proud bearing provide stability to his family.

Did he really love Helga? Can one really know such a thing? How, for example, did Mr. Binger know that he loved his wife? One should ask him. Up to now he had always provided a very solid answer to every question. Helga could consider herself fortunate to have such a father. His own father had died so long ago that he had had only very little influence on his life. But even if he had lived longer, if he were still alive, would that really make a difference? He had not really been a very remarkable man. One could sum him up in one word: civil servant. Always he had done his duty, punctually, just as the railroad expected it. Never had he asked why a new regulation replaced an old one, never had he complained when he was obviously taken advantage of, and he could not even remember that his father had every raised his voice, even if he had done something naughty as a child, which in every other family would have earned him some corporal punishment.

Quite some time ago, when he was 18 or 19, he had once asked his mother whether his father had ever had any ideals, or perhaps dreams that he had shared with her. Perhaps some that she could not fulfill. She had not quite understood his question. ever since her son had some college he seemed to have ideas that she did not really understand. But then, she did remember that when they were first married, they were both still quite young, and he had been interested in the labor movement. But as time went on he had lost interest in going to meetings and distributing leaflets and being part of any sort of organization. She recalled that she had once asked him about it and he had said something about having responsibilities now and that he didn't hold with all this liberal pie in the sky stuff they talked. And as for herself, she could remember that when she was a young girl she had had a crush on some movie actor and loved to dance. She guessed all girls go through this sort of kid stuff.

Well, no wonder that his parents could not have served as a model for him. As a matter of fact that was also true of school. There had been nothing that had really interested or moved him especially and none of his teachers had ever made the effort to get to know him. Maybe it had been his own fault and he should have tried harder. Some evening after a while he should ask Helga about this because he was sure that her father had been a model for her. Yes, that would be a good subject matter. He was sure that it was always useful to have a sort of list of subjects in mind that you can bring up when you are going to live with another human being for the rest of your life. It didn't have to come up right away.

Only now did he notice that his water had really grown very cold. He was sure he had never been in the tub quite so long before, but it was of course possible that this would be the last time, and besides he really had a lot to think about today. The white cottony surface had long since turned into an ugly gray film, the icebergs had melted, and the island had vanished in the sea. He could now see his own body like behind a dirty window.

When he dried himself he knew that tomorrow he would marry would Helga and he would try to live up to her father's expectations.

HAPPY BIRTHDAY

It does not happen often that a mistake is made in heaven, but once upon a time it did happen with rather catastrophic consequences. It happened like this:

Quite some years ago the news had reached heaven that the theologians on earth had now successfully proven to mankind that there is no such thing as a hell or such a creature as the devil. Since the thought of a hell and the devil had always been rather disagreeable to all men and women, people accepted this proof with immense joy, and even the most sinful member of the human race now expected that upon their death, they would immediately be transported up to heaven.

Of course, in heaven they knew about the real truth of the matter, but long experience had also taught them that truth was not something that was taken very seriously on earth. Thus, steps had to be taken to prepare for an enormous crush of arrivals at the gates of heaven, and that, unfortunately, was a problem that could not be solved so easily. Most of the angels were already fully employed in their job as guardian angels, while the younger and newer ones were busy learning to play the harp, which required many hours of practice to make certain that there would never be any disharmonious sounds heard in the spheres.

It was clear that this was a problem that had to be taken for a solution to St. Peter, who was not very enthusiastic about this new assignment, since he immediately recognized that the answer would require a major adjustment in his book-keeping. In fact, a reliable source revealed to us that he was heard to mutter, "Oh man", which in heaven is the equivalent of a rather strong curse, and was not at all characteristic for him. He knew enough about those theologians on earth, that he had reason to fear that not only those who were passing away from day to day would be knocking at the gates of heaven, but that a movement would also develop to make certain that souls from the past who had clearly been possessed by the devil would be declared to have the equal opportunity to enter the pearly gates. Thus, added to the crush would be criminals, crooks, Communists, and even so-called Liberals. How could the administration possible deal with an orderly registration and assignment to this or that cloud?

Luckily, being omniscient, St. Peter immediately realized that there was only one answer: Computers! For those who had watched him eagerly for an answer, this was a sad moment. The old gentleman had, of course, experienced many changes during his long tenure as gatekeeper. It had not always been easy, because at heart heaven was kind of old-fashioned. But something as radical as computers, going mechanical, electronic, that really seemed the last straw! The worst of it was, that he had foreseen it when it was discussed by the Heavenly Committee on Inspiration which had agreed by a vote of 15 to 2 to permit human beings "the inspiration" to invent this device.

Nevertheless, there simply was no other way out, and just as once upon the time in Paradise, one had once again to bite into the sour apple. A giant computer center was installed on a certain cloud and since it was operating day and night, that lovely soft cloud soon turned darker and darker until it seemed quite dirty, so that one could not even see it any more from earth. Only astronomers were puzzled by those regularly flickering lights, which had never before been discovered among the stars. And, of course, there was a rather ominous humming sound, not quite like an approaching thunderstorm or tornado, so that nobody in heaven wanted this cloud anywhere in the neighborhood.

Naturally, after some rudimentary instruction, all available angels had to work overtime until this monster would finally create some sort of orderly file system, and initially even the saints were urged to volunteer their time for the project. Luckily they acquiesced to help out just as soon as they had completed their regularly preferred assignment. For those who do not know it, we might add that all saints have the privilege of herding the sheep on a particularly beautiful meadow.

Who could possibly be surprised that with all of this hustle and bustle something was bound to go wrong? Those of us who are still living on earth have heard it often enough when a bill shows the wrong amount, when a message did not reach us, when an announcement is misspelled, "It was the computer". Naturally, we have to harbor this belief that the computer is fallible, as long as we believe in the infallibility of human beings. Once again, in heaven they know better: computers make mistakes if operators make mistakes.

For that reason it is painful to have to report that for once a mistake was made in heaven. Let us avoid naming names, let it suffice that we know that one of the older saints grew increasingly tired from this unaccustomed work. He was working on a project that would register all those souls who were still living on earth, and the data entered on their files included not only the date of birth, but also the date of their predetermined demise. It was just about sunset, and the saint's head began to droop while the setting sun reflected brightly on his halo. Just for a mini-second he was blinded, but that was enough to determine the fate of a certain Henry Goodheart, a man who was naturally still alive, 52 years old, and someone who bore his honorable name with considerable justice.

Henry lived in a small town, was happy with his loving wife and two industrious sons, who by this time had presented him with six grandchildren. All of his life so far had developed according to plan. Only one time in his life he had traveled away from his town to the big city, which had been much too crowded and much too noisy for his taste. If it had not been for this fatal mistake in his fate, he would have lived on happily for another 19 years, peacefully growing older as scheduled.

Of course, for a while everything proceeded as expected, small town life continued with only minor changes, and only a few people noticed that Henry Goodheart hardly seemed to age at all. Good genes most of them thought, and quite a number of his contemporaries rather envied him. At the party for his seventieth birthday he even romped around with his great grandchildren, and gave no indication that he was as winded. Late in the evening when the guests were quite exhausted and wanted to go home, he grew rather petulant and complained that it seemed to him that they had not really meant to celebrate him. Naturally this remark did not sit too well with a number of his friends, who had worked hard all day to prepare for this party.

In fact, partying seemed to have become his major preoccupation these days. There was no wedding, no christening, and no burial anywhere in a ten-mile radius where he did not participate energetically. No wonder, that he also concluded, after his wife had passed away two years ago, that he should marry again, and as it turned out, there were a number of widows who soon hinted that they were quite prepared faithfully to cook and care for such a young-looking vigorous man. Small wonder that nobody was surprised when Henry chose a rather vivacious lady of only 36, who indicated quite publicly that she had found it difficult to resist such a virile suitor, and therefore nobody was really surprised with the announcement of the birth of a young daughter. Henry himself had long since ceased to listen to all the hints and jokes about his youthfulness. No doubt in his mind that all this talk was really born of envy.

The years passed and in this small town were very little ever changed, people had gotten used to the phenomenon of Henry Goodheart. The children from his first marriage passed away at the proper time, and their children had already become grandparents themselves. That young second wife sadly had also died at age 57. Rumor had it that she simply had been unable to keep up with the vigorous pace of her husband's life. Once more therefore, he took a wife, his third one, but since the younger women were all just a bit afraid of him, this time he had to settle for a 73 year old widow, who, however, only two years later gave up the ghost. Since life with her had been rather boring from his point of view, he did not consider her passing a tragic event.

What was much more disturbing for him when he was in his late 90s by the calendar, that there were only two 88-year-old men in his acquaintance left to whom he could talk about the good old days. When these men eventually also passed away, Henry suddenly felt very lonely and deserted. So many new generations now separated him from his original family, that the various offspring frequently simply forgot that he was a relative and failed to invite him. Thus he wandered around the Alike a lost sheep, and often enough it happened that he was regarded in a rather resentful manner, since it seemed to the good citizens of this industrious little town that such a vigorous man had no business just hanging around.

But when he reached his 125th birthday, life once again seemed wonderful and exciting, indeed almost too exciting for a 52-year-old. His pastor discovered the birthday by chance as he perused some of the parish documents, and he told a reporter about this old gentleman who looked so very young, and thus the story reached the paper of the district capital, and in the end it was hardly surprising that every television channel invited him for interviews. Soon the whole world discussed this remarkable phenomenon, and more than one ruler from this or that country would send him a birthday telegram. Presents rained down on him from everywhere, and it is understandable that everyone wanted to know the secret of his longevity.

Not surprisingly, certain firms were quick to exploit him. Which toothpaste, which soap, which breakfast cereal, which beer, even which cigar and many other products were responsible for his oh-so-golden-old age? Naturally, he was well paid for all of those endorsements, although up to now he had never even heard of most of those items he happily advertised. To him one of the most enjoyable parts of all of this was the fact that he was now often photographed, surrounded by exceedingly pretty young women, frequently even in rather scanty attire. Sadly, however, they just laughed when he tried to flirt with them in the manner in which he had learned to flirt. And in fact, none of this sudden fame lasted for very long. Companies began to realize that the general public believed they had been exposed to a huge hoax because nobody believed that Henry was really as old as they claimed, so that manufacturers of face creams that guaranteed the disappearance of wrinkles, just as used by Mr. Goodheart, soon had to defend themselves in courts of law against the accusation of fraud.

Thus life soon became very quiet around Henry again. The small town into which he had been born in the meantime had grown into a good-sized city where nobody cared about anyone else, and so he lived on in complete anonymity and terrible loneliness. Very quickly he learned that when he did come in contact with other people to keep silent about his history, because people then simply considered him to be deranged. Once, he read in the newspaper about a certain historical event as described by a well known scholar Henry, who had lived at that time, realized that the man had not only distorted the facts, but also interpreted them in a totally inappropriate way. When he wrote to the university in the hope that there might be some interest in actually talking to a witness of the events at that time, his letter remained unanswered. After all, these events had happened about 175 years ago, so obviously the offer was simply a joke by some graduate students. Henry, however, was terribly disappointed, because he had hoped that in this way he might still be of some use.

Once again, he was now 185 years old, he was discovered when an antiquarian searched through some documents left by a church that had ceased to exist long ago. But nobody believed his announcement that records indicated the existence of a 185-year-old man except for the owner of a well-known circus. The result was that Henry received a letter asking whether he might be interested in joining this enterprise as a sideshow attraction. Although he's still harbored some prejudices against those rootless Gypsies, as he had always called them, he accepted the offer. The idea to travel the world now seemed rather attractive and would surely be preferable to loneliness. But when he arrived at the appointed day at the winter quarter of the circus, he was rather brutally dismissed immediately, because, of course, nobody believed his age since he still looked 52. Only the bearded lady seemed to show some sympathy for his predicament, advised him to apply some makeup and for the show put on a long white beard. He thanked her for her well-meant advice, but he could not get himself to lose his natural dignity in such a manner.

Nevertheless, this encounter with this lady had its good side, even though Henry never was to know about it. It so happened that this bearded lady died 12 years later, and since she had lived a decent, honest life in spite of her affliction, she really did go to heaven. Once arrived, she soon became quite popular (her beard had, of course, fallen off. There are no angels with beards as, I am certain, you know) because she had traveled much, seen many things, met many strange people. And so it happened that one evening she told about her meeting with Henry Goodheart at the very moment that St. Peter happened by. Naturally, he too joined in the laughter, but later in the evening, when he was about to go to sleep on his cloud, somehow that matter did not let him rest. Quickly he calculated that if this poor soul should really be of that age, he must have been one of the first ones who had been registered by computer. Of course, St. Peter was endowed with a quite extraordinary conscience, which is how he had achieved his illustrious position in the first place. In spite of some touches of rheumatism, he got up again, determined to find the answer.

Surely we can imagine his shock when he discovered the truth. Immediately it became clear to him that someone had punched a 5 where there should have been a 2 under the rubric "fate", and that in this way a man had been condemned to an almost eternal life. Quickly he called for a new card from one of the angels on duty, and by his own hand entered the proper information, and even made sure it found its proper place in the master computer.

Henry, of course, knew nothing about all of this when sad and depressed and all alone he celebrated his 198th birthday. For so many years now his most fervent wish had been release from this endless life, so much so that he had even considered the idea to bring it about by his own hand. But each time he had shied away from it, since he considered it to be a rather severe sin.

Sighing deeply he lay down on his bed; as so often, tears were in his eyes. At last he fell asleep, and when he woke up he heard the most wonderful music, and found himself surrounded by many of his old friends who slapped him on the shoulder, and embraced him, and gave a great demonstration of a heartfelt welcome as they all sang "Happy Birthday to You!"

JUSTICE

Most likely you have never heard about a certain Oskar Kille, whose misfortune made him unwittingly into a mass murderer. Truly, his sad fate would have deserved to appear in large headlines in every newspaper of the civilized world, but actually it was the newspapers and T.V together with the police that were responsible for the fact that the public was never properly informed. Inside information has revealed that they were afraid they might create a precedent.

But since we reject all censorship and firmly support freedom of the press, and since it is all past us now anyway, there really should be no reason to continue to keep the matter a secret.

Actually the case did not even begin as a murder case, but merely as an attempted robbery for the most understandable reasons. Oskar needed money. Of course, we know that in our circles it is the general rule that in a situation of this sort one looks for a job, or if one already has one, and it isn't enough, one goes to a bank which stands ready to help out for the payment of interest on a loan. However, Oskar had never considered work to be fun, and so he had never had a job, and his experience with banks consisted of a failed attempt to reach a safe through an underground tunnel. Surely you understand now, our Oskar was a typically criminal type of the sort one can recognize immediately from a mile away.

Up to this point in his life he had not killed anyone, but that was really only an accident. During his career in crime he had more than once beaten up his victims rather mercilessly, so that it can only be regarded as a miracle that none of them had died. Even in the considerable number of fights in which he had been involved when he was just a kid, and also later, fights which had as often as not been brutal because he always carried a knuckleduster, nobody had ever been killed.

Obviously, Oskar was not a very agreeable citizen, and one can only marvel that in his 38 years he had merely spent twelve of them in prison. Most likely he had been luckier than one would wish upon such a type, that he had never been caught during his most lucrative break-ins or his most brutal fights.

But this time things were different. Oskar had gotten together with several of his pals in a dive where they all felt comparatively safe, and they had cased a job they would do tomorrow. Insurance company or something like that. Naturally, as always, Oskar had a big mouth in their planning, and because the profits promised to be quite enormous, he fully expected that from tomorrow on he would live the easy life. In fact, he was ready to start now, tonight. "Hey, guys, let's have a drink all around. I'm buying!" he shouted. "Let's start the good life right now." The suggestion met with enthusiastic approval, except that the guy who owned the joint had heard this sort of thing many times before. He knew well enough that not all plans hatched here worked out successfully. That was why he wanted the money right now. No credit! Oskar considered this demand an insult to his generalship, and was immediately ready to beat the hell out of the man. Thank heavens three of his pals just barely stopped him.

It was never altogether clear whether he was really insulted, or whether he knew full well that he had no money for this treat in his pocket. What was clear was the fact that he could not embarrass himself in front of his friends.

"O.K., O.K!" he shouted. "Start pouring. I'll be back in a sec." After all, getting a few bucks had never been much of a problem, and so he stormed out the door to enrich himself at the expense of the next solid citizen in his way.

Sure enough, it didn't take long until he found him, or rather, he found her. Just about seventy steps away he saw a young lady who was obviously on the way home. "Somewhat unusual," he thought, "at least in this neighborhood, and at this time of night. Ah, what the hell..." and he went straight up to her and asked for her purse. After all, he was in a hurry; his friends were waiting. She looked at him rather startled, and then she began to cry. "Damn it," he thought, "she's even pretty." But for a professional that shouldn't make any difference. Break of the game, you just can't let yourself be distracted. Too bad for her though.

Can you imagine Oskar's surprise, when the young lady not only seemed to ignore his outstretched arm, but even rather expertly swung her pocket book in such a way that it landed precisely on his already rather bulbous nose. In amazement he stared at her, his arm still stretched out in front of him. Only slowly he became aware of the fact that a considerable amount of blood was pouring over his lips, and when he reached up to wipe his nose, he recognized right away that it was broken.

Now surely this would not have had any severe impact on his beauty, things like that had happened to him before, more than once, but then always only in fights with guys like him. But this fragile looking young lady, who by the way suddenly looked very hard, she had attacked his honor. Like a raging bull he snorted with anger and desperation as he bared his blood smeared teeth. Every other human being would have immediately taken flight, if only he would have given the opportunity. At least one might have expected that this young woman, who just moments ago had begun to cry, would go down on her knees and beg for mercy. Not that it would have helped her, because Oskar, in his primitive view of life, had already decided to kill her. Quickly he reached into his pocket to retrieve his trusty knuckleduster, and planted himself with his legs spread out wide in front of her. She retreated, but like a lumbering giant he went toward her step by step, until her back seemed almost to be touching the wall. "Now!!" He strained every muscle in his body and struck a mighty blow in her direction when he suddenly saw stars. Only gradually did he recognize that these heavenly visions were the result of the fact that his head had been   banged into the wall.

Like a stone that is dropped into a deep well, Oskar plopped to the sidewalk. Only dimly did he feel a sharp blow on his neck, and that somehow both arms seemed to have become tied to each other on his back, and had lost their use. The last thing that he remembered was a shrill whistle, and then everything went dark.

Only hours later he woke up again with a terrible headache, but he realized right away that he was lying in a nice clean bed. There seemed to be a bandage around his head, his nose hurt like hell, and his chin was held in place by some kind of contraption. Oh, his good right arm turned out to be in a cast, and all in all he was a mess. When he opened his eyes fully, he saw that at the foot of his bed on a chair was a man in uniform.

"Well, Oskar," the man said comfortably, "so you've come to pay us a little visit again. How do you feel?"

Oskar could only groan.

"Nice girl, Anita, isn't she?" the man said with some irony in his voice." And so pretty, too, don't you think?"

That was too much for Oskar. "Lousy whore!" he grunted with all the strength he could muster.

"Not at all," the man in uniform laughed, "she's the prize package of our division. I would have thought that even you with your primitive mind would have caught on that she is with the police."

Actually Oskar had not considered that up to now. "Man, oh man," he said, "can she ever hit."

"Naw," answered the policeman, "actually not, but she's a black belt in judo, so you don't need to be ashamed of yourself."

Well, it would go too far to tell just what all happened next in detail. Suffice it for us to know that after seven weeks Oskar was ready to leave the hospital, although he still had to go through a few weeks of recovery in jail before he was ready for trial. Unfortunately, his fellow prisoners seemed to know about his bad luck, and wherever he went, he could hear some suppressed giggles, none of which helped to restore his usual good mood. For that reason he could hardly wait for the time when he would go on trial and could defend himself against the charge of attempted murder.

Naturally, as we already know, Oskar had no money and so he could not afford to hire his own attorney. But justice was prepared to take care of cases of this sort, and so the services of a certain Lucas Kleinert were put at his disposal. Lucas was still a rather young man, just at the beginning of a splendid career, through which he hoped to be able to help the suppressed and disadvantaged masses to achieve justice by his brilliant juristic arguments and dedication. This case was, in fact, his first real case for the Office of the Public Defender.

Oskar Kille, of course, did not recognize what a jewel he had on his side, and the young man's idealism merely bored him. Nevertheless, with a somewhat tired voice, he agreed to tell Lucas his life's story in detail, as far as there was anything to tell at all. The defender, however, seemed satisfied, and (unfortunately) slapped him on the shoulder as he assured him that everything would turn out just fine. The meaning of that assurance was not quite clear to Oskar at the time, because he had the dark premonition that this time everything would go wrong, and that surely because of his previous convictions he would be locked up for life as a danger to the general public.

When his case finally came before the court nobody paid any attention, which was understandable. It was a routine matter, attempted robbery and resisting arrest. Only an elderly reporter was present, mostly because his rheumatism bothered him this morning and he was looking for a place to sit down. The charge was read, the nicely dressed lady from the police testified with a charming smile. While she talked, Oskar kept his eyes closed. It all went very fast, and nothing much more was expected from the attorney for the defense except the usual plea for understanding and clemency.

But this is the point at which everyone was wrong. Lucas Kleinert assumed a "lawyerly" position (he had learned it from watching many movies), and with ever increasing emotion in his voice began to recite the life story of his client. He told about the unsettled and broken home conditions under which Oskar had grown up. The father had spent the formative years of his son's life in prison, and his mother had more than once been on the verge of arrest, since in her job as attendant in the toilets at the railroad station, some well-founded suspicion had arisen that she was dealing in stolen jewelry. School also had failed to be a positive and guiding influence on Oskar, who consequently had cut classes more than he had attended. Obviously the system had failed to hold his attention and inspire a love for learning. At eighteen he had had his first encounter with the law when he was arrested for grand theft auto. Following his release from jail, he only saw the world outside for scarcely a year before he was caught during an attempted bank robbery. An additional factor that determined his sentence this time was the charge that he had beaten up his 63-year-old landlady. Luckily the lady had survived, but she would never again be able to walk properly. Nothing was said at the time about another rather brutal fight in which one of the participants lost an eye.

The court and the jury listened in great amazement at this rather detailed recital, which could after all only serve to add to any prospective sentence. Obviously Oskar was an extremely dangerous criminal who should be locked up for the rest of his life. But suddenly there was a turning point in this so-called defense. With a quavering voice, Lucas began to interpret these events.

"But now let us look at this life once again from the human side," he began. "Was it really the fault of my client, that his father was an alcoholic and a criminal? Let us not here try to understand how he came to this point. And don't forget the poor mother. Here she is, lonely and deserted with a small son who embodied all her hopes for the future. Can she also be a father to him? She tries it, she plays football with him in the street (Oskar could not remember that at all), she tries to build an airplane with him from a kit ("Man, oh man!" Oskar thought). But soon she discovers that the financial help from the social agencies is not enough to live a decent life. She is desperate. Some of her friends recommend prostitution as a steady source of tax-free money. But no, she is a decent woman, she wants to be a role model for her son as she earns their meager daily bread, and still try to send a gift of love to her innocent husband in prison. She accepts this menial position as a cleaner of toilets in the railroad station, a job that she carried out with dignity."

Everyone in the courtroom suddenly became aware of the fact that Lucas Kleinert was just now getting a full wind in his sails.

"Just imagine it yourself, Gentlemen. Maybe some of you are also fathers," he started most urgently, And he suddenly seemed to grow by several inches. "Now here is this little boy, left all to his own devices. Why? I shall tell you why," he leaned forward toward the jury as if he were sharing a secret with them. Because the court had condemned not only the father, but the entire family!" Here he paused in the hope that the image would have its desired effect. Then he continued with upturned eyes:" I ask you, Ladies and Gentlemen, should one not expect from a humane society that it now take care of and support generously this poor abandoned mother and child?"

The judge obviously had something on his mind as he stared at Lucas over his glasses and then at his watch. The lawyer did not seem to notice it. "Perhaps you think differently," he continued. "Perhaps you think that it doesn't hurt the mother in wind and weather to go to the toilets in the station and do her duty. But think also of the little child, all alone at home in their dank and dismal apartment. Should not the state at least see to it that such little victims (Oskar liked that) grow up in an airy and sunny environment? In a kindergarten under the guidance of a well trained and loving young kindergarten teacher and the attention of practical nurse? There little Oskar could have played with other children and learned how to live in community with others. Would it really have been asking for too much for the state to bear the cost for the education and development of this poor little lost soul?"

Oskar suddenly became aware of the fact that tears were running down his cheeks. For the first time he thought of his lost youth which up to now had always seemed so wonderful and exciting with all those harmless thefts and little frauds. It had always seemed to him lucky that no parents were ever around to interfere with his life. Besides, he had never considered these times as lost years. After all, that was when he had learned his trade. Had he really missed something? He was certain that he would soon have gotten the best of that pretty young thing in the kindergarten. And as for the other kids, well even then he had been stronger than most.

Still, Lucas went on. "I am certain you now see, Ladies and Gentlemen, or at least you should see, it is not Oskar Kille who ought to sit here as the accused. He himself should be the accuser." And now he continued in this vein, he sketched how the teachers in school had failed to interest Oskar in learning; how they had based their teaching on people like Shakespeare and Milton and all that sort of out-of-date thinking, instead of touching upon the problems that had a bearing on Oskar's life. Were not they also guilty? "Were not employers guilty because they had failed to hire Oskar because to them he looked and acted like a typical criminal? Is it right of society that it looks only at external features, rather than to search for the soul of the applicant? (Oskar tried hard to remember whether he had ever tried to get a job?) And finally, here is this little boy who lives in those wretched surroundings, but he is not insensitive to the rest of the world that only cares about things, about luxury. Who of you has not sinned, not yielded to temptation? Can't we understand that he would borrow a car so that at least for a few hours he might have the illusion that he is also one of the lucky ones in the sunshine of the world?

Was it not wrong to send him to jail just in these formative years, rather than to guide him to an apprenticeship program? Surely here he would have learned a trade that would some day have helped to support him and make a desperate attempt to rob a bank unnecessary."

Perhaps as you read about these events you are not moved, but those who were present in the courtroom were obviously shaken by this insight into a wasted human life. The lady court reporter wept unashamedly and probably missed some of the testimony because she continually had to wipe her nose. The eyes of the ladies and gentlemen of the jury were visibly red as if inflamed, and the judge had taken off his glasses and frequently wiped his face with the sleeve of his robe. Even the representative from the attorney general's office seemed to suffer from frequent fits of coughing. We should also note that Oskar's ugly face had suddenly been completely transformed. He looked radiant in the total enjoyment of the recounting of his own suffering. One could now almost think of him as handsome.

Finally, finally after three hours the defense seemed to come to a conclusion. "It must now have become perfectly clear to you," Lucas Kleinert asserted, now with great and dignified composure, "clear who is the guilty party.

Not this man, Oskar Kille who has been sinned against more than he has sinned. No, not he, but you, Ladies and Gentlemen! Because you here represent the social order that is responsible for the crimes that have been committed on this unhappy man here. You have abandoned him on his journey on the Road to Damascus. Only a judgment of 'not guilty' can save him from becoming completely disillusioned. Do your duty! Free him as a demonstration and admission of your own sense of guilt."

With these words ringing in their ears, the jury withdrew. Oskar was taken to a small room where he was to wait for their return. There was no doubt in his mind now, that in no more than a couple of hours he would be back with his friends. Perhaps even in time to pull something or other, because by now he was really short of funds. Lucas Kleinert seemed exhausted and rested his head on the table.

We do not know just what took place in the jury room. We only know that when after three hours the bailiff knocked at the door to find out whether he should bring something to eat, all they asked for were 4 boxes of Kleenex.

At eight o'clock in the evening the judge had begun to wonder about the length of the consideration of guilt or innocence. The building was already quite empty when he directed the bailiff to try to listen at the door, to find out whether the discussions were still ongoing. Since he heard not a sound, he very carefully opened the heavy door just a crack, and then he saw the catastrophe. All those present in the room were lying on the floor, each with a little round hole in his temple. Dead! On the table he found a letter addressed to: Mr. Oskar Kille. When the letter was opened and read to the judge it stated, "The victim Oskar Kille is innocent. Our vote is unanimous, and we ask for his forgiveness. We also demand that the state compensate him generously for the years he spent in prison." The letter was signed by all those on the jury, and below the signatures was written in quite a shaky hand: "We also petition that the lawyer, Lucas Kleinert, be forever barred from appearing before the court. He is a dangerous man!"

ABEL

For how many years had Abel been sitting in that old green chair? No, sitting is not the right word. He was crumpled, or was it slouched down, so that he and the chair seemed to be one. How do you count time when time no longer means anything to you? There had been a time that was now a vague memory when it had meant something. Now you are 21, now you are a man! At that time he had thought, "It's like a new life, like being finally born to be you. Now the world is really open to you." Strange that he could remember those moments, even though only vaguely, but he could not really recall what came next. Had he then entered that world eagerly, even joyfully, or just a little bit afraid? Why did he even think of it now when he was so very far away from that time? Ah, yes, of course, then he had had something to look forward to. To do something, to be something, to mean something. That sort of moment would never come again. Had that world welcomed him, opened its arms wide to greet him as though it had been waiting for him for a long time? Had he been a success? Had his life meant something to anyone? Even to the world at large? — Why could he not remember? Perhaps there had been nothing worth remembering. But did even that matter when you are more than a hundred years old? ...'more than...` How much more?

He could feel a presence. Someone had come to do something. To feed him...with a spoon... like a baby? To wash him with a sponge, very gently as though he might break apart if there were too much pressure? To put him to bed because it was time for bed? As though that mattered. Day and night no longer meant anything. His vision had become so clouded that he was barely able to distinguish night from day. Just as his hearing made it hard for him to distinguish individual meaningful sounds. Someone handled him, obviously said something to him with those patient almost singing sounds that sometimes made him recall his earliest awareness of his mother.

No, this was more than one of those routine events that reminded him of what was left of his sense of time. He was lifted from his chair, hands fussed with his clothes. Feebly he tried to stand.

"Please let me sit again," he thought, and really, they did, but not in his ancient green chair that had so much become part of him that it seemed as though it had been made to his specifications just like a tailor-made suit.

He felt movement, movement without any effort on his part. This chair had wheels and he could feel someone behind him that caused the movement. Ah, yes, he could identify what was happening. He would soon get a whiff of fresh outside air and then be lifted chair and all into a van. That was something that happened ever so often and such journeys generally wound up in the hospital. As a matter of fact, he had come to look rather forward to such visits. They were a change from the daily routine of nothing. He came in touch with some sort of machinery there, something was being measured and analyzed. There was a vague remembrance that he might have had something to do with machinery when he was still alive... He smiled at the thought that he had verbalized often enough when he was first taken to this retirement home. People would ask him questions, many of which he then could still answer, and frequently he would wryly give the answer with the prologue "when I was still alive." Humor was important. He had always thought so, and for quite a long time in his later years it had helped him., But not any more. Maybe some things were still funny, but they had something to do with actual happenings or with things neither of which were still part of his life.

He must have nodded off. It happened frequently in the middle of a thought. Where was he? This was not the hospital, too many people all around him, whispered conversation, ever so often he could feel that someone patted him on the shoulder. Very gently, obviously afraid they might bruise him.

What now? What was this sound? Yes, music, strong, powerful music, organ music. Church music! It suddenly seemed as though a whole floodgate of memories had been opened. When he was very young his mother had taken him along with her to church. He was bored most of the time and his mother had to keep reminding him to respect what was happening, to assure him that some day he would learn what all of this talk meant and how important it would be for his entire life. As the years passed he had learned how to behave in church, but he never understood his mother's attachment to it. What he now recalled was the fact that church had been a sort of social thing, like a kind of club whose membership made you respectable. Ever so often during all those years of going to this or that service he remembered what had moved him most was the music, especially later in life when he had been in churches much larger than the one his mother had gone to. He was not a heathen, and he often enough thought he might delve more deeply into these matters just as soon as he had more time. Somehow he had missed that moment, and after the green chair seemed to have become his home, both his memory and his concentration had begun to fade rapidly.

But not now. He suddenly inhaled more deeply than he had in years to capture a fragrance long since forgotten, the fragrance of a pine tree and in his mind's eye he could even add the colorful decorations that made it come to life in such a special way. He could quite clearly hear and understand the words that told of the birth of a baby, of a new life, and his lips formed the silent words: "a new life"... and again: "a new life"... when his unseeing eyes were suddenly blinded by a glorious light and a chorus of a thousand voices filled his ears. For the first time in years a smile came into his face as he thought once more "when I was alive"!

On the next morning the trash man came to haul away the green chair.

THE SCIENTIST

Eddie Englert is sitting in his garden uncertain as to how he should feel. Happy that it is over? He had given it so many years and so much serious search and effort. Let's see, he is 57 now and he graduated with his degree in Biology with a doctorate when he had been 24. So this problem has been with him for more than 30 years now. His research for his thesis had been on cabbage of all things. Not really a very interesting problem, but that was what his doctor father wanted him to do and if he ever wanted to get that degree he had better do just that. It was not all lab work, the literature dealing with the growth, development, even history of cabbages required consultation. It was at that time when quite by chance he ran into what appeared to be an ancient manuscript. It mentioned a spinacea venecum, a bug or a substance that seemed poisonous. There was no date but a name Maximo Germanum as the scientist responsible. "What is it?" he asked one of his professors. "Nothing important" was the only answer he would get. He insisted "but it seems to be poisonous!" ... "lots of stuff is, just mind your own business and get on with your degree." He did, graduated, got a job quite quickly with a food distributor and from then on spent his life deciding whether this batch or that batch of asparagus, cabbage, tomatoes, apples etc. was safe to eat. Routine work, to be sure, but it paid well enough that he could marry, buy a house, have a family (two boys) and feel comfortable and secure.

Not an all consuming existence until one day at supper; he remember it vividly, it was the 12th of October 1942, when his older son asked," What kind of stuff did you study, daddy, when you were in college?" It seems they had talked about this sort of thing in his class today and Eddie was glad enough to answer. He had actually not thought about this for some time, so he talked about research and tomatoes and it took some time for him to notice that the others around the table had long ago stopped listening to him. Yet not he, because all sorts of memories started to dominate his thinking and even the unfinished business of those former times

Of course the papers covered it and the firm's management assured the public that Its scientific safeguards were the best and that their head scientist even went so far as to look into the future with his private research into the poisonous spinacea venecum. Eddie was pleased, because here was the first public mention of his research. Not for years had he gone to the alumni meeting at the university since nobody much had talked to him. But now that his name and his research had become public knowledge it might just be different.

It was. A few of the fellows smiled and slapped him on the shoulder and said things like "good show". But then one of the men, obviously from an older class took him by the arm and suggested they talk in a corner.

"1 don't think 1 know you," Eddie said.

"Yes, you do and I owe you an apology. I am Maximo Germanum!"

"But, but you are dead" Eddie objected because he could think of nothing else to say.

"It was a joke," the older man explained. "My actual name is Max Hermann and I sort of Latinized it for the joke. We students had been out drinking and eating and I had gotten rather sick with diarrhea so on the next day as a joke we composed this fake document to warn against poisoned spinach. Nobody ever destroyed, it and it never occurred to us it would be taken seriously." So that was it and how should he feel now? Like a fool who has been fooled? Or should he be glad that it is all over and he was free now of his "problem" and he would never have to look at another date. This had dominated his life for so many years, yes, dominated but also filled it out, giving it meaning. What now?

A collection of mini stories depicting the relationship between reality and imagined reality. A number of people face questions such as: 'does he (or she) really like me? Did I misunderstand this event? Is my imagined life better than my real life? How do I? How can I? Should I?'

Obviously life and reality are full of questions and to wrestle with them can be fascinating and often amusing.